DEHUMANIZED

ZANYA YADAV

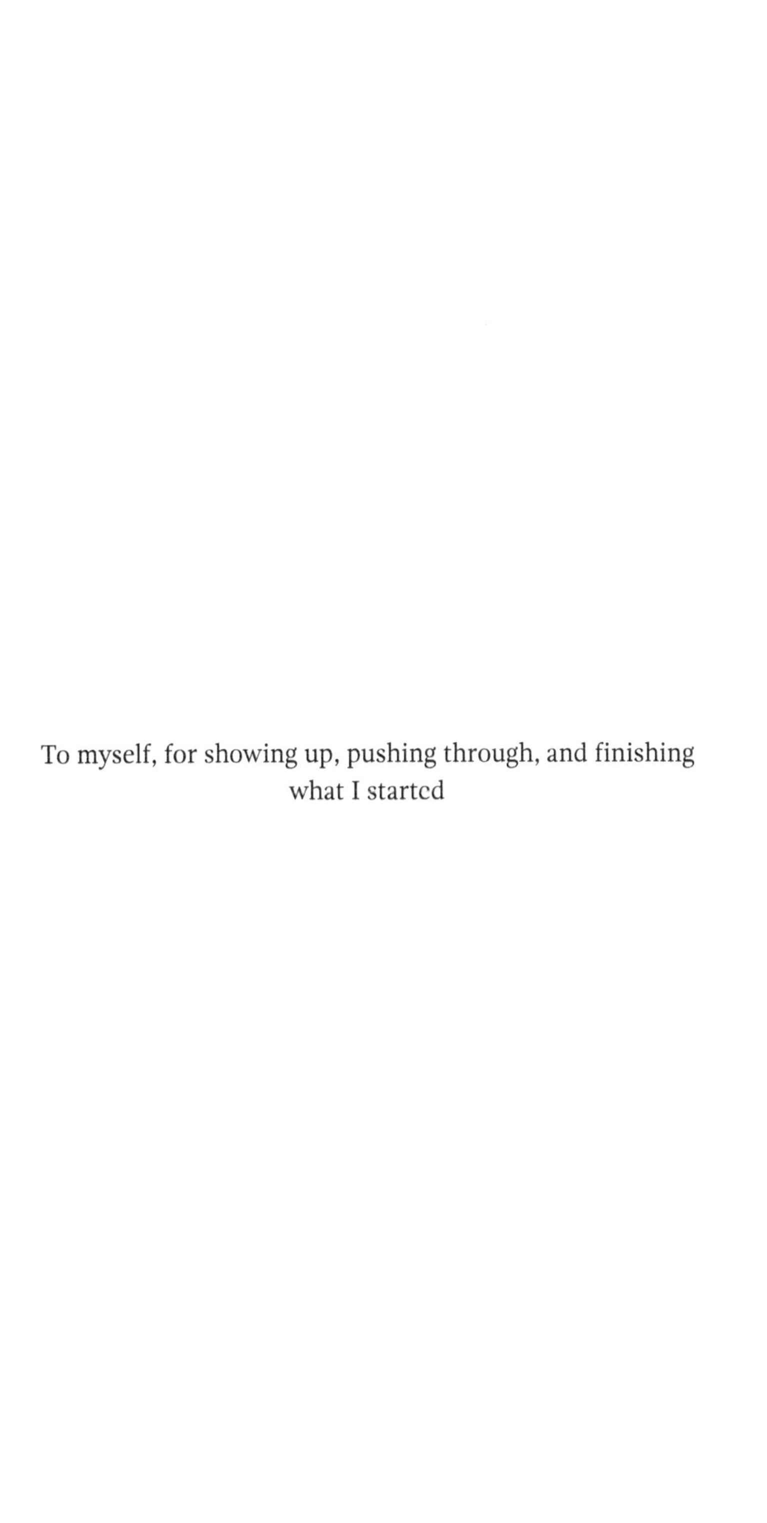

To myself, for showing up, pushing through, and finishing
what I startcd

Contents

Contents

Preface

If you began reading this book you must be wondering what is Dehumanized or what's its relation to the story. Have you ever wondered that there can be something odd, really odd from us humans? It can look like us, possess us and make us do whatever it wants. Maybe it haunts away our loved ones and separate them from us, all at once. This book depicts one of those mysterious stories or myths which you grown up listening to. Story of a girl wanting to lead a normal life like other high schoolers do. Never knowing what awaits for her or her fmily.

Story of a investigation team and it's members, whose lives were getting tangled, wanting to solve the unsolved mysteries, but as they solve one mystery knot, their fingers get tangled more into the web. They sacrificed their social lives, just to reach the end of this story. But little did they know that somehow, they involved themselves in the story too!

Their only problem wasn't that one mystery they were trying to solve, but was two stories going on in the same timeframe as they began joining the connection dots. The dots joined too! but most of the hooks remained independent. It seemed the stories had several ends if they search for them, but they never found any end, or did they?

Let us begin with the story to find out how much pain this creature caused to the possessed ones and their families and the ones trying to collect normal evidences not realizing this case wasn't natural... it was supernatural. The people who were dehumanized, can they be human again? or they become a permanent bridge between the worlds of ghosts and humans?

A question still remains the same within the curious minds of us being humans, do normal people have encounters with ghosts or supernatural powers?

Writer's Message

It's my heartful gratitude to the people out there who are reading this novel, I hope the readers enjoy my story thoroughly, I've tried to give life to the fictional characters being mentioned here.

This novel is a pure work of fiction and hence, the characters and places mentioned in it are not related to reality, the story it carries and the mention of supernatural things and creatures are not proven to be real.

The people who may or may not believe in such things can enjoy the story in their own perspectives.

Thanks to the lovely reader of this work

CHAPTER ONE

NEW HORIZONS

It was a Sunday afternoon Holmes were driving towards a new beginning into their lives, the new horizons. Having the whole family in a car, talking rubbish, having fun and heading towards south-east into the state of Georgia. "I think the clouds look weird today", says Asher. "Maybe you didn't had time for watching any horror tv shows today that's why you're cooking up one story for yourself", soon after Andrea replied. She never missed a chance to poke at her brother. "I think you got enough guts to reply your brother in an insolent way, maybe you should apologize", replied Mrs. Holmes "he just was getting to know the surroundings better and seeking your attention towards his dedication don't let him grow a feeling of despair" she added later.

They were laughing and chatting, lost in their own little world, when suddenly - out of nowhere - a white-tailed deer sprang into their path. Mr. Holmes' reflexes kicked in, but it was too late. The car swerved, tires screeching, and the car careened off the road, plunging into the darkness of the woods. Time froze as metal crunched and glass shattered. Then, silence. "Everyone okay?" Mr. Holmes' panicked voice cut through the stillness, his words trembling with fear. Mrs. Holmes nodded, still trying to process what had just happened, as their children's stunned faces turned towards them, their eyes wide with terror. 'Andrea? Asher?' he called out, his voice cracking, 'are you hurt?' The only sound was the creaking of twisted metal and their ragged breathing.

As they limped up the driveway in their battered car, the family finally laid eyes on their new home. The two-story building stood before them, its worn facade and chipped paint evoking a sense of neglect. A once-manicured garden, now overgrown with weeds, flanked the entrance, while a sun-bathed patio area seemed to be the sole redeeming feature. Andrea's face contorted in dismay as she gazed out the window. "Dad, is this really it?" she asked, her voice laced with disappointment and shock. "It's so...old and ugly!" She turned to her father her eyes wide with incredulity. "You said it was a great place! I thought it would be, like, a beautiful house with a big yard!" Her father, still relieved from their narrow escape, offered a reassuring smile. "It's got character, sweetie. And it's home now. We'll make it beautiful together." But Andrea's skepticism remained, her gaze fixed on the house's uninviting exterior.

As boxes and suitcases spilled into the rooms, the family dove into unpacking and organizing. Andrea, still adjusting to the new surroundings, sought comfort in familiar routines. "Mom, what's my new school like?" she asked, folding a stack of t-shirts. Laurene paused, smoothing out a wrinkle on the couch. "You'll be attending St. Anthony Abbot High School, sweetie. It's highly rated and just a short walk from here." Andrea's eyes narrowed and concern etched on her face. "Will I fit in, Mom? I don't know anyone." Laurene smiled reassuringly. "You'll make plenty of friends, Andrea. You're smart, kind, and beautiful.

Asher will be at the middle school just down the street, so you'll have him nearby too." Asher, now an 8th-grader, looked up from his phone, grinning. "Yeah, sis, I've got your back."

After unpacking the stuff altogether Laurene asked if the kids were hungry. She, then made some fluffy pancakes to assure the reward for helping in for organizing stuff. "You should be prepared for tomorrow, I don't want you to be late for your school's first day", added Laurene while having dinner. "Wait, we have our classes tomorrow and we don't know anything about the students there", said Asher while looking at the dull face of Mr. Holmes. "You were going to stalk them!?" asked Andrea, no sooner did she finished her question than Asher replied in shock "I don't mean that I'm going to stalk anyone as being a popular one myself..." Andrea replied with a smirk "Please, you think being popular in an 8th-grade class of 200 students is impressive?" Asher's smile faltered. "Hey, it's not that hard for me! You're just jealous because you're starting over in high school." Laurene intervened, "Hey, kids, let's not fight. We're all adjusting to this new life together. Andrea smirked, "Sorry, Mom. Just keeping Asher's ego in check." Asher muttered under his breath, "You're just mad because you're going to be a nobody in high school." Andrea's smile was gone, her voice icy. "At least I won't peak in middle school."

As night descended, Andrea slipped away from her family's gentle chatter and stepped onto the balcony, drawn to the twinkling lights of the main road. The stars above mirrored the scattered glow below, and the world seemed peaceful. She breathed in the crisp evening air, feeling the stress of the day melt away. But as she leaned over the railing, her gaze drifted downward, and her serenity shattered. Footsteps, light and deliberate, echoed below her window. Andrea's heart skipped a beat as she tried to peer down, her eyes struggling to adjust to the darkness. That's when she saw him – a man shrouded in shadows, his face obscured by a black cat perched on his shoulder. The cat's piercing green eyes locked onto Andrea's, sending shivers down her spine. A jagged scar marred the cat's sleek fur, and its unblinking stare seemed to hold a sinister intent. Andrea's comfort vanished, replaced by unease. She swiftly closed the window, her mind racing with questions, and retreated to the safety of her bed, but the cat's haunting gaze etched in her memory.

The morning sunlight streamed through the windows as the family went about their routine. Laurene expertly juggled cooking breakfast and helping Asher and Andrea prepare for their day. Asher devoured his pancakes, discussing his plans for the school day with Andrea. As they stepped outside, the crisp air invigorated them. The siblings walked together, chatting about their classes, until they reached the four-road merge. Here, their paths diverged – Asher heading left toward the middle school, Andrea right toward the high school.

"See you later, sis," Asher called out, waving.

"Later," Andrea replied, smiling briefly before turning serious. Her mind drifted back to the mysterious figure from last night. As they parted ways, the sounds of the town awakened – cars humming, birds chirping, and distant chatter from students heading to their respective schools.

As Andrea walked through the school hallways, heads turned in her direction. Whispers and admiring glances followed her, making her smile. She was used to the attention, but it still felt nice. In her classroom, Andrea scanned the room for an empty seat. That's when she spotted a girl sitting alone, her eyes cast down, and her shoulders slumped. Something about the girl's isolation tugged at Andrea's heart. Andrea walked over to the girl, her long hair swaying with each step. "Mind if I sit here?" she asked, smiling warmly. To her surprise, the girl looked up, her eyes flashing with skepticism. "Why would a beauty queen be sitting with a nerd like me?" Her tone was laced with self-deprecation and a hint of bitterness. Andrea's smile faltered for a moment, but she recovered quickly. "Because I think everyone deserves some kindness, regardless of labels," she replied gently, taking a seat beside the girl.

The girl's expression softened, and she introduced herself as Clara. As they began to talk, Andrea discovered they shared a love for literature and poetry. Clara's eyes sparkled with surprise. "You're not what I expected." Andrea chuckled. "What did you expect?". "A shallow girl, only caring about looks and social status," Clara admitted. Andrea leaned in. "I'm more than just a pretty face."

As the final bell rang, signaling the end of the school day, Andrea gathered her belongings. Suddenly, a tall, handsome figure emerged from the crowd. Mike Lewin, the most popular boy in school, commanded attention wherever he went. His chiseled features, piercing blue eyes, and charming smile made every girl weak in the knees.

Girls nearby couldn't help but stare, their faces reflecting a mix of admiration and envy. Whispers spread like wildfire: "Mike's talking to Andrea!" "Who's the new girl?" "She's so lucky!" Mike approached Andrea with confidence, his athletic build and effortless charm radiating an aura of assurance. "Hey, I'm Mike Lewin," he said, flashing his famous smile. Andrea's heart skipped a beat, but she maintained her composure. "Hi, Mike. I'm Andrea."

Mike's eyes crinkled at the corners. "I've seen you around. You're new here, right?" Andrea nodded. "Yeah, just moved in." "I live nearby, in the same colony," Mike said. "We should hang out sometime." Andrea smiled warmly. "That sounds great. You can visit my house anytime." Mike's grin widened. "Definitely will."

As they parted ways, Andrea couldn't help but notice the jealous glances from her classmates.

Mike leaned against his locker, exchanging whispers with his best friend, Alex. Alex raised an eyebrow. "Dude, what's with you and Andrea? You've got every girl in school chasing you, but you go for the new girl."

Mike shrugged, a hint of a smile playing on his lips. "I don't know, man. There's something about her."

Alex chuckled. "The great Mike Lewin, smitten. Who would've thought?" Mike shot him a warning glance. "Shut up, Alex." "Seriously, Mike," Alex said, "what's holding you back? You're Mike Lewin. You can have anyone." Mike's expression turned thoughtful. "That's just it – I don't want anyone. I want Andrea. And I want it to be real." Alex nodded. "Then do it. Hang out with her, get to know her. Tell her how you feel." Mike's eyes sparkled with determination. "You're right. I'll make it happen."

The next day Andrea leaned in, whispering to Clara during class. "Oh my god, I'm still reeling from yesterday. Mike Lewin talked to me!" Clara's eyes widened. "What? That's amazing! What did he say?" Andrea's cheeks flushed. "He just introduced himself and said we should hang out. But seriously, Clara, he's the most handsome guy I've ever seen, and he's the most popular guy in our batch... Why would he talk to me?" Clara grinned mischievously. "Maybe he found you attractive?" Andrea's face grew redder. "That's crazy. But... I have to admit, he's really attractive, and I love his aura too." Clara nudged her. "So, you like him! You should tell him!"

Andrea shook her head. "No way, I don't think I can do confessions. That's too scary." Clara chuckled. "Come on, Andrea! You're always so brave. What's holding you back?" Andrea sighed. "What if he doesn't feel the same way? I'll make a fool of myself." Clara's expression turned serious. "You won't know unless you try. And think about it – Mike Lewin, interested in you? That's a once-in-a-lifetime chance!" Andrea smiled wryly. "You're not helping, Clara!"

Andrea took a deep breath, gathering her courage. She scanned the hallway, spotting Mike leaning against his locker, chatting with friends. She walked towards him, her heart racing.

As she approached, Mike's eyes locked onto hers, and he smiled. "Hey, Andrea!" Andrea's nerves dissipated slightly. "Hey, Mike." His friends nodded in greeting before dispersing, leaving Mike and Andrea alone. "So, what's up?" Mike asked, his eyes crinkling at the corners. Andrea shrugged, trying to appear nonchalant. "Just wanted to say hi." Mike chuckled. "Glad you did. I was thinking, maybe we could grab lunch together today?" Andrea's heart skipped a beat. "That sounds... great." Mike grinned. "Awesome. I'll meet you at the cafeteria at 12:30?" Andrea nodded, smiling. "I'll be there." As they parted ways, Andrea felt a rush of excitement. She couldn't believe she'd mustered the courage to talk to Mike again. At lunchtime, Andrea arrived at the cafeteria, her palms sweating. Mike was already there, saving her a seat. "Hey," he said, standing up as she approached. Andrea smiled, feeling more at ease. "Hey."

Andrea went on shopping later that evening but when she saw the moon she quickened her pace as the sun dipped below the horizon, casting long shadows. The air grew colder, sending shivers down her spine. As she turned onto her street, the chill intensified. She sensed being watched. Suddenly, a figure emerged from the darkness. The man with the black mask.

"Andrea," he whispered, his voice low and ominous, "come with me. I'll give you a new life."

Andrea's heart racing, she stepped back, but her feet felt heavy. That's when she saw the black cat, its eyes glowing with an unnerving intensity. Fear consumed her. Andrea dropped the bag and sprinted toward her house.

She didn't dare look back.

Breathless, she burst through the front door. "Hey, sweetie! Welcome home," Laurene said, concern etched on her face. "What happened to the groceries?" Andrea forced a smile. "A dog snatched the bag from me." Laurene frowned. "Oh no, are you okay?"

Andrea nodded, hiding her trembling hands.

Andrea's heart still racing, she locked her bedroom door and approached the table, her eyes fixed on the grocery bag. It sat innocently, as if never leaving her grasp. A chill crawled up her spine. How did it get here? She distinctly remembered dropping it. With a surge of panic, Andrea rushed to the bag, her hands trembling. She grasped the handles, flinging it toward the open window. The bag sailed through the darkness, landing with a soft thud on the ground below.

With breath caught in her throat Andrea peeked out the window. The black cat emerged from the shadows, its eyes glowing like embers. It approached the bag, mouth open wide, and clutched it in its jaws. As the cat vanished into the darkness, the bag seemed to disappear with it. Andrea's mind reeled. What was happening? Was she losing her grip on reality? The room seemed to close in, shadows twisting into menacing forms. She felt watched, vulnerable. Suddenly, the window creaked shut, the sound echoing through her room like a sinister whisper. Andrea spun around, but she was alone. Or was she?

Andrea's mind reeled as she tried to shake off the feeling of unease. She couldn't focus on her homework, her eyes drifting toward the window. The cat's glowing eyes haunted her. Restless, Andrea decided to distract herself by organizing her family's old trunk in the attic. Amidst yellowed letters and faded photographs, a dusty envelope caught her attention.

"Confidential" was scribbled on the seal.

Curiosity piqued, Andrea opened the envelope, revealing a newspaper clipping: "Local Family Tied to Mysterious Cult." Her eyes widened as she read about her own family's involvement in a sinister organization. "Mom, what's this?" Andrea demanded, marching downstairs. Laurene's expression darkened. "Where did you find that?"

"The attic. What's going on, Mom?"

Laurene hesitated before speaking in a hushed tone, "Your father... he was part of a group. They believed in summoning powers beyond our world." Andrea's eyes widened. "What powers?" Laurene's voice trembled. "Dark forces. They thought it would grant them control, protection. But it consumed your father."

Andrea felt a chill. "What happened then?"

Laurene's eyes filled with tears. "His brother disappeared, after which he resigned from the group but before resigning the contract he went on a last voodoo where he accidently made a mistake and a ghoul entered from the world of demons to ours, it is said he had a cat with him he looked for humans to devour the human flesh and to produce more ghouls of his kind by sharing his own blood with other humans. I thought I'd protected you from all this, but... it seems the past is catching up.

CHAPTER TWO

Unexpected Encounter

Mike sat with Alex in the school courtyard, looking concerned. "What's up, Alex? You sounded urgent." Alex leaned in. "I overheard Andrea talking to Clara yesterday."

Mike's interest piqued. "What about?"

"Andrea was gushing about you," Alex revealed. "Your looks, your personality... She's clearly smitten."

Mike's face lit up. "Really?"

Alex nodded. "I think she likes you, man. You should confess your feelings."

Mike's eyes sparkled. "You're right. I've been wanting to tell her."

Alex grinned. "About time! Take her on a walk, romantic setup, and spill your heart out."

Mike chuckled. "You're a genius, Alex."

Alex shrugged. "Just helping a friend. Now go, make it happen!"

Mike took a deep breath, determination coursing through his veins. Later that day, Mike approached Andrea after class. "Hey, want to take a walk with me?"

Andrea's smile lit up. "Love to."

As they strolled through the park, Mike's nerves dissipated. Andrea's laughter and easy conversation put him at ease. They reached a serene lake, watching the sunset.

It seemed like he was waiting for the right moment to confess how he felt "Andrea," Mike began, his voice sincere, "from the moment I met you, I felt a connection. You're intelligent, beautiful, and kind." Andrea's eyes locked onto his.

"I think I'm falling for you," Mike confessed. "I wanted to tell you sooner, but... I was scared."

Andrea's cheeks flushed. "Mike, I—"

"Please, let me finish," Mike said, his heart racing. "If you don't feel the same way, I understand. But I had to take the chance."

Andrea nodded, "I would surely think about this" she stated her words followed by a polite smile.

Later that evening when darkness encountered their walk, their eyes met a small, black figure sitting beside the road. Mike approached the figure, it was a cat. Andrea's voice trembled as she whispered, "Mike, I think we should go back now..." But Mike, oblivious to the danger, continued to coo over the cat. Andrea's eyes frantically scanned the darkness, her heart racing with every snap of a twig. The cat's presence confirmed her worst fears - the masked man lurked nearby.

Suddenly, Mike's back stiffened, and he froze. "Andrea, come see," he whispered, his tone a bit calm. Andrea's legs refused to move. She knew what was coming. The cat's eyes locked onto hers, glowing like lanterns in the darkness. Andrea's breath caught as Mike held the cat.

Behind her, the masked man emerged from the shadows, his presence seeming to draw the very air out of the atmosphere. Andrea's scream lodged in her throat. He slowly pulled Andrea into the cold darkness behind her and not even a word did she uttered at that time. It seemed like her words were burning in her throat, every time she tried to speak.

Suddenly the cat scratched mike's chest and went off his hands, running towards the same direction as where the man took Andrea. "Strange…. Isn't it?" asked Mike with hands on his bleeding chest and turning around in the hope for reply. Mike's eyes scanned the darkness, confusion etched on his face. "Andrea?" he called out, taking a step back. "Where did you go?" He spun around, expecting her to pop out from behind a tree, laughing. But the silence was oppressive.

"Andrea!" Mike shouted, panic creeping into his voice. He dashed through the park, calling out her name. The only response was the distant hum of crickets and the faint rustle of leaves. Mike's heart racing, he retraced their steps. Had she wandered off? Was she playing a prank? The cat's scratch on his chest throbbed, a nagging reminder of the strange encounter. "Andrea, this isn't funny!" Mike yelled, desperation seeping in.

As the darkness closed in, Mike's fear intensified. Where was she?"

He ran to the nearest police station, panting for air as he spottted an officer and rushed towards him. He reported the officer and told him everything he knew but Mike's frantic explanation fell on deaf ears. "I'm telling you, officer, she just vanished! One minute we were walking, the next, she was gone!" Officer Brennan raised an eyebrow. "Convenient story, kid. How did you convince Andrea's parents to let her go on a walk with you?"

Mike's frustration boiled over. "They didn't know! She wanted to get out for a bit, and I thought it'd be harmless. We were just talking, and then... and then she disappeared!"

Officer Brennan's tone turned accusatory. "You expect us to believe a 16-year-old girl just vanished into thin air?"

Mike's voice cracked. "Yes! I'm not lying! it was all so surreal."

The officer's expression hardened. "Save the fantasy for someone else, kid. We'll be investigating you, not some mythical figure. Give me her parents number" he held out a paper for Mike to give him necessary details about her family members and his too.

Afte taking the phone numbers, Officer Brennan called Andrea's parents and informed them about the complaint Mike Lewin brought to him.

After some 10 minutes, Andrea's parents, Laurene and Johnathan, arrived, their faces etched with worry and anger.

Laurene's voice trembled. "Mike, what have you done with our daughter?"

Mike's eyes welled up. "I swear, Mrs. Andrea's mom, I didn't do anything! She just vanished! and I couldn't find her anywhere!" John's face reddened. "You're going to regret this, Mike."

Officer Brennan intervened. "Let's take Mike in for questioning."

Mike's world crumbled. "You don't believe me... no one believes me. But you cannot investigate a person below the age of 18 without their parents, so I wish to call my father before having any other accuse" said Mike confidently.

Mike's hands trembled as he sat in the cold, sterile interrogation room. His father, Jenipher, stood firm beside him. Officer George Brennan's gaze bored into Mike, his voice dripping with skepticism. "So, Mike, you expect us to believe Andrea vanished into thin air?" Mike's voice cracked. "It's the truth, Officer. I'm not lying."

Brennan's expression twisted. "Save it, kid. We've heard it all before." Jenipher's eyes flashed with anger. "That's enough, Officer Brennon. My son deserves respect."

Brennan's smile was icy. "Respect is earned, counselor. Your son's story sounds like a fabrication."

Mike's frustration boiled over. "It's not a lie!" Jenipher's face reddened. "That's enough. We're leaving." Brennan's voice rose. "You're not going anywhere until we're done here." The air was thick with tension as the standoff continued.

That's when Edwin Simpson, the head of the investigation team got the perfect cinematic chance to show up. Imagining continues reasons for the bread-jam given in his lunchbox instead of something interesting. "Sir?" asked George by ruining the most important thing currently going inside an investigator's mind. He surely was devastated but got more important tasks and mysteries to solve rather than the bread and jam.

In a low voice, "What's the matter?", he asked. "That boy is trying to waste our time by telling illogical stories about how a girl vanishe." Says Brennan, somewhat mockingly. In a cold environment surrounding Mike with heavy footsteps coming in his direction got him chills right down his spine. He panics again hoping if this guy trusts him, or else expecting for a long speech about what you should and shouldn't do at this age. To his surprise everything he heard was "send him to juvenile until he spills the beans".

Jenipher panicked "Hey Mr.! you can't take Mike to Juvenile, he isn't the culprit, and until you prove that he's not going any...." "Are you going to stop me? silly you because this is my work and I don't show any piece of mercy!" says Simpson. "Let's go and take that boy with you we'll get him enrolled tomorrow itself" he added later.

The butcher's mysterious meat

"I'm done with my work today so would you like to join in for a dinner?" Eve asks. "Only if you'll be paying." Mockingly replies George. "We'll be having dinner at my place so everything's on me" she added later. They both sit in the car as Brennan drove away from the office.

Eve and Brennan exchanged uneasy glances as they approached the butcher's shop. The sign creaked in the wind, reading "Fresh Meat" in dripping red letters. Inside, the butcher's demeanor sent shivers down Eve's spine. His face hidden behind a stained apron, he gruffly asked, "What can I get you?"

"1 pound of chicken, please," Eve replied, handing over the money.

The butcher's gloved hands moved swiftly, wrapping the meat in brown paper. As they walked home, Eve noticed Brennan's silence.

"Hey, are you okay?" Eve asked.

Brennan nodded with his eyes fixed on the package. At home, Eve unwrapped the meat, and her scream echoed through the halls. Brennan rushed to her side, and together they stared at the horror before them. A severed human hand lay on the counter, flesh torn, fingers brutally severed. Eve's vision blurred. "Oh God... what have we bought?" Brennan's face ashen, he whispered, "We need to go to the forensic lab and call sir Simpson." Suddenly, the phone rang, shrill and ominous. Eve hesitated, her hand trembling as she picked up.

"Hello?"

A low, raspy voice spoke, "You shouldn't have bought that meat."

It horrified Eve to an extent that she dropped her latest model phone. She was stun and was left with no words to reply with her feet shivering and throat being choked by shock, she was served with some water by Brennan. "Let's leave already" these were Brennan's last words until they reached the laboratory. He was in the same shock as Eve was going through but he had to look strong enough to handle her.

Eve's eyes widened in horror as she stared at the DNA test results, her mind reeling with the unthinkable truth. Brennan's concerned expression mirrored hers as she stammered, "It's... it's Andrea's hand." The room seemed to spin around them, the air thickening with an unspeakable terror. Eve's hands trembled as she dialed Andrea's parents' number, her heart heavy with the devastating news. Laurenc's voice, laced with anxiety, answered on the first ring. "Eve, what's wrong?" Eve's voice cracked, "Laurene, I... I need to tell you something." Brennan's supportive grip on her shoulder steadied her. "It's about Andrea," Eve continued, each word feeling like a betrayal. "We bought meat from the butcher... and it was her hand." The line fell silent, as if time itself had stopped. Laurene's anguished wail pierced the stillness, followed by Jonathan's stunned murmurs.

Brennan's face had paled, his eyes fixed on Eve with a mixture of shock and dread. "This can't be happening," he whispered, his voice barely audible. Eve's gaze met his, sharing the same unspeakable thought: Andrea might be dead. The butcher's sinister grin flashed in Eve's mind, his gloved hands handling the meat with an unsettling familiarity. "We have to call Sir Simpson" announces Brennan.

[later that evening] "You have mistaken this can't be that girl's" suggested Simpson with a pale look on his face. "But this DNA test report won't be lying", says Eve defending her forensic report's reputation while handling the test results to Edwin. "And I think she might be dead by now with her other body parts lying in opposite directions of Savannah." George stated his intuition. "Or maybe any horrors of the town captured her?" says Noah, the junior Inspector working with Edwin Simpson, he was a traditional guy having his superstitions in the back pocket of his cargo pants. "Your rubbish is scratching its way through my brain cells, how can anything like 'the horrors of the town' capture a girl and separate her hand from her and gift that to a butcher to sell it off to any Detective and a scientist who would end up telling this to a fool like you who would be making a joke about any horror thing!" shouted Simpson is a single breath while looking at Noah in expectations that he would react in a tone of guilt.

To his surprise Nova reacted back something weirdly this way- "How would I know where the butcher got that piece from?" At that time everyone could tell that Noah was checking the patience level of Edwin.

In no time Mr. and Mrs. Holmes were called to inform the new evidence found, just to divert the little mind of Noah from Simpson. After around 5 minutes the doorbell shattered the stillness, announcing Andrea's parents' arrival. "We'll find out who did this," George promised, his determination forged in the fire of horror. As they sat, numb and shell-shocked, Eve's mind whispered a haunting question: What other atrocities lay hidden in the shadows of Savannah?

After discussing the situation for about an hour and half it was almost 2 AM. Holmes' were sent to their home, for their safety Noah drove them home. Everyone was tired as their sleep cycle stretched on for too long. Simpson and George went home by the time reached 2:15. Eve was offered a ride by George but she denied as she had to complete her reports by the time. She was feeling so addicted to the mystery that she hasn't been so addicted to any case before *as 'normal cases had natural cause and reasons but this one didn't have a natural hand behind it'* she talks within herself. She was tired but as the coffee machine didn't work she got furious, as her mind diverted from her work she turned down her face towards her wrist watch.

After having a tiring three hours of research it was almost 5:30 AM and now she decided to leave the office and drive safely to her home. It was still dark in Savannah and she found her car tires punctured but it was not a normal incident as it had a clear look of intentional action. She was frustrated and decided to leave her car parked in the office's basement and have a walk down street. The streets were empty, "people don't like waking up early these days" she guessed.

CHAPTER THREE

The Evil Awakening

She suddenly felt the presence of something near her taking deep breaths, matching the rhythm of her footsteps, as she walked deeper into the fog the image began to clear. She choked with confusion and fear the figure was resembling something which wasn't supposed to be here, having both the hands present, "How could that be possible, holy shit" were her last words before crawling her steps forward in the same path where Andrea vanished.

It was a girl having both arms but a face resembling the person who was supposed to be dead. "Andrea?" was the only thing Eve asked to that black shadow. To her surprise it didn't answer. She began to take steps after steps slowly towards her, shaking with fear and her feet trembling badly that she couldn't even walk properly. As Eve rushed toward Andrea, relief washed over her, but it was short-lived. Andrea's eyes, once bright and warm, now gleamed with an otherworldly intensity. Her smile twisted into a grotesque grin, revealing razor-sharp teeth. Eve's joyous call faltered as Andrea's hands transformed into razor-clawed weapons.

"Andrea, what's wrong?" Eve pleaded, stumbling backward.

Andrea's response was a guttural growl, her body lunging forward with inhuman strength. Eve's screams echoed through the deserted road as Andrea's claws ripped her flesh, sending blood spurting onto the asphalt. The black cat emerged from the shadows its eyes fixed on Eve with an unblinking stare. As Andrea's teeth sank into Eve's wrist, the cat began lapping up the spilled blood, its tongue darting with an unnerving delicacy. Eve's agony intensified, her vision blurring. Andrea's drinking intensified, her eyes flashing with an eerie glow. The cat's presence seemed to fuel Andrea's frenzy, its tail twitching in rhythm with Andrea's sucking.

Suddenly, Andrea's grip relaxed, her eyes clearing. For an instant, the old Andrea flickered back. "... run," Andrea whispered, before the demonic presence reclaimed her. Eve stumbled away, tripping over her own feet. The cat vanished into darkness, leaving behind a trail of blood.

[The following day]

Eve's abrupt leave of absence sparked whispers among colleagues. Her relatives' vague explanation - "health issues" - only fueled speculation. Simpson, ever the skeptic, sensed secrets lurking beneath the surface. As team leader, he summoned a meeting to discuss the Andrea's case. "Eve's contributions were invaluable," Simpson began, his voice tinged with concern. "Her sudden leave raises questions. We need clarity." Noah frowned. "Could it be related to Andrea's disappearance?" Simpson nodded. "Possibly, let's go to Lewin's house and let us see if we find something related to Andrea." The team reluctantly agreed.

Meanwhile, Eve lay hospitalized, her mind shrouded in darkness. The incident's trauma had shattered her psyche, silencing her brilliant scientific mind. Depression's heavy veil suffocated her. Visitors were few, conversations hushed. Eve's isolation deepened.

Next morning Simpson with his team reached Lewin' house at seven. The investigation started the moment they reach, Noah started checking the green belt (obviously without permission to do so) "Have you gone out of mind?" asked Brennan while pulling his collar out of the bushes. "What are you up to? This was my favorite shirt!" announced Noah, pulling his shirt off from Brennan's hand and walking towards the door.

George Brennan's firm knock echoed through the stillness, prompting Jenipher to open the door, a mixture of curiosity and apprehension etched on his face. "Simpson, what brings you here?" Jenipher asked, stepping aside. Simpson's expression was grave. "We're investigating potential evidence. May we enter?" With reluctant consent, the team dispersed. Brennan's trained eyes scanned the kitchen, homing in on a translucent droplet on the counter. His heart quickened – saliva, freshly shed. "Noah, over here," he whispered urgently. Brennan's eyebrows arched as he collected the sample with precision. "Bagged and tagged. Let's keep this quiet for now."

After some half-an hour, their covert operation complete, the team retreated to the laboratory. Anticipation hung heavy as Simpson processed the DNA. Hours ticked by, each minute elongating the suspense. Finally, Simpson emerged, his face a mask of stunned disbelief. "The saliva belongs to Andrea." Brennan's eyes widened. "But that's impossible. We assumed she was... gone."

Here comes Eve!!

Eve's fragile frame stepped into the laboratory. a month's absence etched on her pale face. Colleagues exchanged warm smiles. Relief evident in their welcoming voices. Simpson, Brennan and Noah rushed to her side, supporting her weakened physique.

"Eve, we've missed you," Brennan whispered, eyes crinkling.

Her gaze drifted, silent and haunting, as if the trauma still lingered. Vocal cords, once sharp and authoritative, now trembled, producing barely audible whispers. George Brennan guided her to a stool, concern etched on his face. "Easy, Eve. Take your time." Dr. Patel handed Eve a steaming cup. "Herbal tea, for strength." As Eve sipped, Simpson briefed her on the breakthrough. "We found Andrea's saliva at Mike Lewin's. The DNA... it's anomalous. Regenerative cells, unlike anything human."

Eve's eyes widen, horror resurrected. Memories burst forth: that dreadful night, Andrea's resurrected form, both hands intact. Yet, the butcher had sold them Andrea's severed hand the previous evening. A chilling realization crept in: Andrea's transformation defied mortal boundaries. Eve's voice, barely audible, sent shivers. "Andrea... alive?" Brennan's nod confirmed her darkest fears.

Simpson's grave tone deepened the unease. "We suspect Regeneration, reanimation... this transcends science." The laboratory, once a sanctuary, now felt vulnerable. Eve's thoughts reeled: What monstrous entity had Andrea become?

It was 3rd of December, Eve was still working on that DNA piece, how it worked? What could be the pros and cons? Why did this happened to be? Were some common questions to be answered. It was a Sunday afternoon, a holiday for team, Eve was still working. Brennan however called her, but she didn't pick it up as she was too busy with her work to think about any other task to be done. But Brennan was tensed as she never missed any call from him "should I try it again?" he asked to himself before calling her second time after his first call made 2 hours ago. "She didn't pick up this time too!" he exclaimed surprisingly, "should I go check on her?" he asked to himself.

No sooner did he started his car he got a phone call from the security officer checking on their office gate. "Hey! Is everything alright there?" asked Brennan "No I just called to inform that my day shift ends here and the officer from the night shift department didn't reach here" he said "so.... Do you have the keys with you?" asks Brennan "Yeah I have them" he replies "Wait there I'm coming you can hand them over to me" Brennan suggested. "How about I give them to Miss Riley?" he asks. "Wait what? Is Eve there in the office?" asks Brennan. "Yes sir! Why are you asking anyway? Isn't she allowed here?" he asks. "No! I didn't say I have problem with that you give her the keys alright? See you later" Brennan hung up.

"So, is she really there? Still working on that thing, I think she didn't have a good breakfast otherwise why is she ruining a holiday?" he asks to himself. He thought she might be at home but instead she was still working at the office's research center.

The research center's nocturnal silence shattered as Andrea burst through the glass door, shards crashing onto the floor. Eve spun around, her eyes widening to the figure which now, stood before her. Andrea loomed, eyes blazing with unnatural intensity, the black cat perched on her shoulder. The feline's gaze locked onto Eve, its eyes glowing like lanterns in darkness. The cat leapt onto the laboratory table, sending equipment and samples crashing. Its low-pitched meow resonated through the room like a mournful dirge. Eve recoiled as Andrea seized her neck, fingers tightening like a vice.

"Where's the DNA?" Andrea hisses, her breath cold against Eve's ear. Eve's voice trembled. "I... it's stored securely." Andrea's grip intensified. "You'll produce it, or suffer." The cat's claws swiped, sending tubes and petri dishes shattering. Eve's world narrowed to Andrea's unblinking stare. Just then, Brennan's voice echoed from the corridor. "Eve, are you here?" Andrea's eyes flashed. "Your savior approaches. I'll return for that DNA."

Releasing Eve, Andrea vanished into darkness, the cat disappearing with her. Eve crumpled, gasping for air. Brennan rushed in, finding Eve on the floor, her face ashen. "Eve! Oh God..." He sprinted for water, returning to find Eve still breathing heavily.

"Eve, what's happening? You vanished without explanation, and now this. Your erratic behavior's killing me." Brennan's grip on Eve's hand tightened, his eyes blazing. "Talk to me! You're shutting me out. I thought we trusted each other." Eve's silence only fueled Brennan's desperation. "That night, you discovered Andrea's hand. Then, sudden leave. No calls, no messages. Your colleagues thought you quit." His voice cracked.

"Today, I found you lying on the floor. What connects these events? Mike Lewin? The supernatural DNA?" Brennan's anger softened, replaced by gentle urgency. "Eve, I'm here, share your burden." Tears brimmed in Eve's eyes as she met Brennan's pleading gaze. Her voice barely above a whisper, she began. "Andrea's transformation... it's not human. Regenerative cells, unnatural strength. I saw her severed hand reattached." Brennan's expression darkened. He began with -"Tell me everything."

You remember a month ago before I took that leave for a month and when I called you saying that I am working late night today? If you remember that is the night I was attacked by Andrea for the first time, her both hands were in front of me even though her right hand was not expected. I got scared but at that time I did not know the reason behind this, later I found out there were regenerative cells present in her DNA that meant she could regenerate and probably that was a regeneration when she grew out her right hand back. I didn't want to tell anyone about this so that's why I came to research on that topic on a holiday. I'm sorry I didn't even tell you and thought I can handle that myself even though I knew deep down that I needed help.

"So that's what happened and you didn't even bother to tell me?" Brennan asked dramatically. "Yes" with a sigh she replied. After a few minutes the conversation got normal and that's when Eve tried to bring in something interesting for this moment. Brennan sat beside Eve's hospital bed, monitoring her recovery. Eve's gaze drifted to his, her eyes sparkling. "George, thanks for your help," she whispered. Brennan's expression remained neutral. "Just doing my job." Eve's smile hinted at deeper feelings. Brennan shifted uncomfortably, focusing on his notes. "Rest, Eve. You need it. "Eve's voice softened. "Your presence makes me stronger." Brennan's response was curt. "Glad to help." Unspoken emotions hung within her. Eve's adoration contrasted with Brennan's detachment. Eve's thoughts whispered: Why can't he see my love? Brennan's silence confirmed he was not interested in nonsense.

Silence broke when Brennan's phone rang at 2 AM. He read the name as Sir Simpson on the phone without wasting any time he picked it up and asked "Hey Sir is there anything I can help with you at this hour?". "Just stop that already, I know I am calling you late night this doesn't mean that you are allowed to behave manipulatively!" exclaimed Simpson. "I just called to inform that I want both you and Eve at office tomorrow at sharp 6 AM she is not picking up my phone maybe will pick yours, so come with her because we are going to talk to Holmes' for the information about their background and some personal details about Andrea" he added later. "Okay! I'll tell Eve to come at 6AM in fact I myself will accompany her" he ended the conversation by this. "Why didn't you tell him that I am with you?" Eve asked as she was awake by the noise. "Do you want to share about Andrea's transformation into something weird and regenerative?" he asked calmly. "Not now, I mean I guess so" she replied in rhythm after his question. "Then if I had told him that you were with me, what reason could I plot at that moment?"

"Thanks for saving me, you came at the right moment" repeated Eve. "It was totally a coincidence. "But I think if I wouldn't have come then maybe we already know where the Road not taken led for that moment!" exclaimed Brennan. "Now you should rest tomorrow we are going at Holmes' for investigation, not for any searching job but for just talking about their background and Andrea's personal life, I bet they are hiding something that could be the biggest clue for this case".

"I remember it I was having a cup of coffee but I felt cold even though I was wearing my expensive natural wool hoodie coat. By the way it was limited edition! Okay so coming back to the main topic for which I bothered you this late night was that when I spun around, I felt shivers down my spine! I saw a black cat out of now where in my private bedroom. The irritating fact was I don't own any cat neither I wanted to have a cat, especially a black one as they were too scary to adopt and too

black to find at night, jokes aside I dropped my cup of coffee in shock, but I regret it till now... it was made in Japan! Coming back to my problem... that cat scratched me! And went out of the window licking my blood off from its claws. Of course, I didn't mind him drinking my blood... but I want at least 5 dollars for my expensive blood drops. Are you going to extract my 5 dollars from that cat or should I consult any animal hunter for my work to be done? Nevertheless, I'm leaving this work to you I live in third old street just inform me the updates but let me tell you one more thing that cat had green eyes like emeralds and a scar like thing on its stomach. I'm telling you if I find that cat I am going to kill him right away, but I am not going anywhere in accuse of murder..."

"Is this man out of mind?" asks Simpson to himself. "He called me late at night just to show off his things with old price tags still hanging on them otherwise why would he remember the cost of each and every thing! I won't disturb him and let him live happy life in his materialistic world and talking about his so called most expensive blood... I'm not going to find any black cat for just extracting 5 dollars from him and who cares about anything so illogical?" he talks to himself. "Wait a second... did I inform Noah that we had to meet tomorrow in office at 6 AM? I don't think so...but I think he is having a night shift, it's okay, I don't need him for now.

"Can you think of a murder happening late at night or we can say early in the morning at 3 AM! I can't believe that... I was on night shift near that area but I didn't find anything suspicious. His window was open, but he lived on fifth floor and I don't think anyone would climb through pipes just to murder or steal something, the murderer anyway didn't used the stairs too, I myself checked the security cameras of that building. It wasn't a suicide either, he was having scratches all

over his body but his finger nails were so short that they can even grow under his skin, anyways he was wearing a hoodie coat of natural wool and I think he was working late at night that's why I saw a cup of coffee spilled on the floor with the cup broken you must come here and see the crime area and you'll find yourself in confusion too!"

"I can't believe this! how many crimes are going on in this city these days!" exclaimed Brennan. "Should I check it out myself or take Eve with me?" he asks to himself. "Are you not feeling sleepy?" Eve asks him.

"Anyways what's up with Noah? He was doing night shift this day right? Did he find something suspicious?" asks Eve one by one so relentlessly that she even forgot the questions she asked before the last one. "Maybe we can go and check that out ourself?" he suggested. "Should we inform Sir Simpson? Let it be I don't want to disturb his sleep cycle" she says. "No problem I will call him, I'll set the scores equal as it was half an hour ago when he disturbed me from my sleep cycle!" exclaimed Brennan.

"Hey Sir Simpson sorry to call you late at night but we have got a neighborhood murder case I'll meet you right after 10 minutes at the Third old street." he said. "Hmm interesting just 10 minutes ago I received an annoying complain from the same street..." doubted Simpson as he didn't agree to digest the coincidence.

After some 10 minutes which went in rush and confusion for Simpson it was the time to climb up to the fifth floor, lift was under construction. "Didn't supposed to be managing with a poor building manager who don't even have an elevator by now?" exclaims Noah. As they reached the floor, Simpson was traumatized by the look of the surroundings. "a cup broken lying on the floor with coffee spilled and scratch on the dead body which was wearing a hoodie coat made of natural wool... but it surely has something different from my assumption, if he's the same guy who called me then he is not having any price tags on his things, it means he remembers the prices of the things he purchased" Simpson thinks while maintaining his gaze onto the dead body. As the person's friend, who was his neighbor rushed in, was stopped and told that he was not allowed in that area. "Interesting... this Japanese cup seems to be broken just beside the location where he died it means... he got a minor shock before attack, was it because of the black cat he saw?" murmurs Simpson.

"Excuse me mister that isn't a Japanese cup it's a normal roadside cup that I gifted him for his birthday a week ago! And can you tell me what's going on here?" his friend exclaims doubtfully. "Hey mister you are not allowed to come in I warned you before so you can wait outside the crime scene until we come outside!" says Noah scolding that man.

"Wait a second, Sir, you mentioned a black cat a while ago and how did you know that man saw a black cat a while ago just before his murder?" asks Eve impatiently in order to confirm some of her doubts. "This man coincidentally called me just before his murder as he was talking some nonsense, I didn't believe him and nor was I interested in his stupid nonsense that's why I hung up. But I didn't assume this would happen, it was totally an accident." Says Simpson. "Hey sir do you know any details about that cat?" asks Eve as she was getting nervous as time passed by. "Yes, he did tell me the cat had green eyes and a scar on her stomach and some more nonsense" he says with a sigh. No sooner did he finished his sentences than Eve started to have abnormal coughs and she started sweating badly that's when Brennan realized that it was the same cat who came with Andrea twice to attack

"There's no way we can find the killer!" announced Eve. "Did we find the killer or we can say the one who abducted Andrea? No, right? So, we cannot find this person too, in both the cases a black cat appeared, they're all so mysterious to fit in any logic behind them in our minds." She added later. "Maybe it was just a mere coincidence?" suggested Simpson. "No, it totally wasn't!" she forced her intuitions. "Now only thing you should be grateful for is that by god's sake this person didn't turn into a monster!" Brennan whispered in her ears.

CHAPTER FOUR

CRIME HOTSPOT

It was just after 2 hours when the team reached Holmes' at 7AM after completing the basic murder case formalities and reports. As the bell rang, cold shivers run down Holmes family's spines. They were scared to answer any of the question that were to be asked. Suddenly they began to form some excuses which they would be using while the investigation being going on. The cops were thinking to ring again but stopped with uncomfortable environment where the beats of heavy footsteps matched with the rhythm of their breathes, drawing closer and closer towards the gate, and finally the door was opened with some scratchy noises. "Welcome Sir!" as Mr. Holmes greeted them with two words and gave them a signal to come inside.

"The house was strange as if it was not dusted from the past 15 to 20 days. The furniture was also not well maintained as Termites had eaten them from inside and made them a hollow piece of wood. The lanterns were a bit old fashioned but I think I can manage with them and as I moved further, I saw Mrs. Holmes drinking a cup of green tea while sitting on a brown coffee colored sofa with some 2 to 3 pin cushions lying on the sofa. Their faces were dull and the dark circles near

their eyes were darker than any being I've ever seen! As we asked about another Child, their son, they told us that they sent him to a country side hostel so that he can be out of danger but they themselves didn't decide to shift as the property was of their ancestors and they didn't want to sell it off just because one family member was missing and 'we had fear of being on missing posters too', they told me." {A diary entry made by Noah later that evening}

They were offered some green tea by Mrs. Holmes but they decided to continue the meeting as a professional one. "Don't worry we are not bribing you to be soft in this question session!" exclaims Mr. Holmes with a terrifying look yet a smile on his face. "No thanks, so, shall we begin?" Asks Eve with a polite tone and face expression. "Did your family had any relations with anything mysterious... you know what I am trying to ask about..." Simpson says softly. As the Holmes' weren't expecting that question to be asked on the first number in the sequence, they were terrified with sweats already surrounding their faces. "N... No, why would we be in connection with any horrors" Jonathan answers quickly with a fake smile. "Ahh... I see" replies Simpson manipulatively. "Anything else sir?" asks Laurene. "Why are you guys in hurry? Is there any family function that you are missing right now and want to get rid of us this early?" asks Brennan doubting on their face expressions. "No sir! We are totally fine with you all staying here for next half an hour" he replies. "We don't have much time either so we'll be here questioning some more topics and then we'll leave, is that fine with you?" announces Brennan. As the conversation got deeper and deeper Simpson saw nothing but an uncomfortable aura around the Holmes'. He suspected maybe they are trying hard to hide something with no traces of proof that could hold them guilty for anything they've done in past or are going to do in mere future. "Let's go then we are just wasting our time!" announces Noah in frustration.

After coming back to their respective homes, finally they felt relieved, just guessing so, waking up to the news of any murder which was just near the night shift duty area of Noah and the person before being killed also called Simpson. All that happened in the time span of 12 hours, tiring! Isn't it? But this was just nothing before the challenges the team was about to face...

It was evening by now and Eve was ready to go back to her lab as it wasn't the time to waste over your sleepiness for too long. She grabbed her car keys before coming out of the basement a green shiny tint followed her eyes, they were like eyeballs but were too large to belong to any human. The moment she understood the situation and rushed towards the exit of the colony was the feeling of realization that something very familiar watched her getting out of her place to reach her destination. "How can this thing follow me everywhere I go? Now how the hell did that cat find my home address!" shouted Eve sitting in her car in frustration and out of fear of being in an encounter again with Andrea.

She was scared as she opened the lab door slowly, I think she was expecting a guest... actually Andrea, to be sitting, to settle the scores this time. All that she found was a post it notes on her lab wall with print of claws onto it. It informed Eve – Holmes' are hiding their past, the thing because of which I became like this! I want you to help me, Riley! I can't endure this pain so the moment you find me next time... can you do me a favor? Can you keep a sharp, very sharp knife with you? So that you can stab me and end my pain right away? ~ Andrea" As she read the request her eyes were filled with tears of grief. "Poor creature, wants to end her life, there is no doubt that I can't even imagine how much pain she is going through. But I would surely end her pain but by not Killing her but instead making her a pure human again!"

Eve promises to herself. After thinking about what Andrea wanted to say in the first line she came to the conclusion that she should surely go to Holmes' one more time as she knew that when Andrea was a human she got to know something really scary and breath taking before her dehumanization that forced Andrea to get her justice and to help her to get out of this matter quickly so that she doesn't risks her life over anything dangerous like what Andrea was going through now.

"Hey Brennan, I want to show you something really good that would help us through this case can you come over to the lab, I promise this time I did found something which would be worth of taking your breath away" types Eve. When Brennan received the message, he didn't reply. Actually, he was so happy and excited to see that piece of clue that he forgot to even answer her messages.

After a while a firm noise of footsteps strike into Eve's ears. As she spun, she saw Brennan, his walking rhythm was weird he was hopping and jumping a little bit with happiness on each step. The moment he saw her he asked right away "Now, where's that thing you were eager to show me?" he asks impatiently. "Just read this and you'll get to know..." she replies while handling the paper to him. He stood there and read that single piece for about 10 to 15 minutes. "I see... the doubt I was having on Holmes' was not my mistake of being too suspicious but it was actually true!" recalled Brennan.

"So... shall we go again tomorrow and show this note to them and ask about the thing they were hiding from us?" she asks. "Why not? We'll go there tomorrow itself" he replies quickly. "But here is my condition that we'll go there without the permission or without giving any information to Sir Simpson, is that alright?" asks Eve as trying to hold the truth again for a little while, she mentioned the reason as she didn't want to bother him for a thing

Or any intuition which was not yet confirmed. He agrees on her condition but tells her that when they confirm anything suspicious and when the truth is unveiled, they would inform their team right away. She also agreed on the term later.

"Every moment in my life became cold at that time when I saw it. No matter if I was happy or sad I would always end up being confused, now, after my 3rd encounter with that cat I am telling you and I am pretty serious there is something really odd about its aura. You know what I mean right? I just am not comfortable since a murder took place in this area and I get scared too easily even if it is a cat, but that wasn't a normal one I've never seen black cats on the streets of Savannah. That makes this situation even worse, maybe it could be pet of the man who is trying to attack me? I don't know about all this stuff as being suspicious is neither my regular task nor my personal interest! That's why I called you to inform I'm so sorry as I know I am disturbing you this late at night but can I get protection? Even if you are willing to send just one cop, it would be more than enough for me. Now I'm cutting my connection for a while and yes, I'm going to keep the windows and doors closed! I just want to spend this night being alive no matter what happens as tomorrow I'm permanently shifting out of the town because this place is turning into a 'Crime Hotspot'!"

"Strange! Another call from the same area. I thought criminals don't attack the same area they have once attacked for sometime, let it be I should maybe just rest as its almost 3 AM and what can happen to a man in merely just 2 to 3 hours?" sighs Noah. "Should I call the cops anyway? Because I can't take risk, maybe, I should talk to one!" Noah talks to himself. "Hey is there anyone on duty near the third old street? If there is someone then please tell him to guard the building of which's address I am going to send you... is that okay with you guys?" Noah politely informs them of his request.

"Nothing was going right here! The moment I reached here I heard some noise of breaking glass, I panicked and led my eyes to there, from where the sound came from. Surprisingly it was just above my head the apartment you had told me to specially focus on. I tried to rush there up as soon as possible but I got stunned by the blood drop that rained on my face after merely a second. I felt chills down my spine, I ran up to the apartment broke into the house through door as it was locked from inside. Th-...then I saw blood everywhere my eyes flashed out! I saw the blood everywhere but couldn't find the person it was coming from after that I don't remember anything but a building manager woke me up next morning and I found myself lying on the bloody floor, he informed me that he found me lying there when he came to check the apartment as its window was broken which was ruining the building's exterior. At first, he thought it was all my blood then when he tried to shift me, I suddenly came to my senses, it was like 10 minutes ago when I woke up and the first thing, I had to do was to inform you about the incident that happened last night!" informed the terrified cop who was sent for protection.

"I never thought a time will come when this city will be holding murders on alternate continuous days!" Exclaimed

Noah. "I shouldn't waste time and inform Sir Simpson about this." He added later. As he called Simpson and informed him about the situation, Simpson got confused about how can two alternate murders happen around the same location? Noah requested him to come and also inform Eve and Brenna about this so that they can join them too. "They both are on leave... they informed me yesterday so I don't think I'll be able to disturb them for today" "well, then no problem... I think we two can handle this by ourselves!" said Noah confidently. "As long as you don't display your IQ level again" murmurs Simpson. "Wait, what are you talking about" Noah asked furiously. That's when Simpson hung up and messaged him to come and meet him directly at the crime spot. "What's with this man now?" Noah complaints.

As they met later on the crime scene, they immediately walked up towards the apartment. They searched the apartment nearly 10 times thoroughly, even called Gracy, the inspector dog, to smell and find out the location of the dead body. But even the dog couldn't find anything.

"Now what should we do with a case where we can't even find the dead body!" exclaims Simpson. "We'll search for it again this evening and if still we are unable to find the man, then I'm sorry we will probably close the case for now..." Simpson Explains "are we going to headquarters now?" Noah asks. "If you would have asked for the office then also, I would've answered you... you call some rooms attached with science lab, headquarters?" Simpson asks by not expecting another silly mistake from Noah.

CHAPTER FIVE

Secret Unveiled

As Eve and Brennan stepped into the Holmes' residence, trepidation settled over them. The ominous silence was broken when Jonathan Holmes ushered them into a dimly lit study. Eve's trembling hands produced the cryptic paper Andrea had penned. Holmes' eyes scanned the message, his complexion paling. Sweat beaded on his forehead as he exchanged uneasy glances with his wife, Laurene. The air thickened with unspoken secrets. Jonathan's hesitation was palpable, fear of exposure warring with obligation. Laurene's gentle touch on his arm seemed to steel his resolve. "We can't conceal it further," she whispered, her voice barely audible. With a deep breath, Jonathan began.

"I still recall those childhood escapades with my older brother. Four years my senior, he'd venture into the woods, leaving me trailing behind. Curiosity gnawed at me, so I followed him secretly. What I discovered haunts me to this day. Hidden uphill, a foreboding temple loomed like a specter. Its air reeked of decay and darkness. I watched, heart racing, as my brother joined hooded figures. Candles flickered, casting eerie shadows. The stench of sulfur and blood filled my nostrils.

It was a black magic ritual, worshiping the devil. My brother's eyes locked onto mine, his gaze commanding silence. 'Don't breathe a word to family,' he warned. 'In return, I'll teach you the dark arts.' His words dripped with an otherworldly allure.

He swore devil worship brought prosperity, surpassing divine blessings. I trembled, torn between terror and fascination. My brother's promise echoed: 'Embrace darkness, Jonathan, and fortune will be ours.' That day, shadows crept into my soul. My brother's secrets became mine. Our bond grew stronger, bound by darkness. Yet, with each passing year, unease gnawed at me. Did I surrender to evil's allure or succumb to sibling loyalty?

Years passed, but memories of that temple linger. Whispers in darkness, flickering candles and an unholy presence seeped into my dreams. My brother's lessons drew me deeper into shadows. Rituals began with innocuous symbols, escalating to blood-stained altars. I witnessed hooded figures conjure entities, their presence choking the air. Eyes glowing like embers watched me.

One night, I saw my brother summon a figure, tall and gaunt with skin like decaying leather. Its eyes burned with malevolent intensity. The air reeked of death. 'Behold, lord,' my brother whispered, 'our patron of prosperity.' The lord spoke in hollow tones, 'Jonathan, embrace your legacy.' Shivering, I vowed allegiance. Darkness enveloped me. But horrors worsened. Nightmares bled into reality. I'd find strange symbols etched into my flesh. Whispers urged me toward unspeakable acts.

My brother's words echo: 'Darkness shields us, Jonathan. Protect it at all costs.' Yet, with each passing day, the shadows closing in, I wonder... have I served the devil or unleashed hell?"

I'll never forget that fateful night. An evil descended upon us, its power surpassing my brother's magical control. The memory still sears my soul. I saw the devil manifest, accompanied by a twisted, glowing-eyed cat. It sprang onto my brother, claws tearing flesh. His screams haunt me. 'Run, Jonathan! Don't look back!' he begged, voice trembling.

I froze, paralyzed by terror. My brother's pleas turned to desperate shouts: 'Go! Let me die in peace!' Tears streamed down my face. I couldn't abandon him. 'Jonathan, flee!' he ordered, his voice fading. 'The devil mustn't find you. Protect our family. It'll slaughter them all.' His words broke me. I forced myself to turn away, leaving my brother to the clutches of darkness. Footsteps echoed through the night as I fled, the sound of shredding flesh and anguished cries forever etched in my mind.

That night, I lost my brother, my guiding light. Grief and guilt suffocate me still. "I weep, recalling his final words: 'Save yourself, Jonathan. Survive. I thought I'd escaped the darkness. Two years after my brother's tragic death, I began anew. Marriage, fatherhood – life's beauty eclipsed pain. My son, born with bright smiles, brought joy. Five years later, Andrea's arrival completed our family.

Serene days passed until that fateful afternoon. My wife and I were downstairs; our children played upstairs. Shattered glass and my son's cries shattered our calm. Racing up, heart pounding, I begged, 'Please, God, save him!' The meowing cat's eerie echo chilled my spine. I reached the second floor, frantically scanning. My son vanished. Despair crushed me. I screamed, wept and pleaded for his return. Andrea, too young to understand, watched with innocent eyes. That day, our world crumbled. The devil found us.

I vowed to shield Andrea. We've moved constantly since, evading the darkness. But now, after all these years, it's found us again. Andrea's transformation, Eve's investigation – the past closes in. My heart races with every creak, every shadow. Will I lose another child? Will darkness consume us all?"

For a moment everything became silent as there was a soft noise of Jonathan weeping about his past and how he, himself ruined the present and endangered the future of his family. It began with his son, and then to his daughter and now it's the turn of Asher, this was the only thing he kept in mind while sending him to a hostel far away so that the devil cannot imagine the presence of his bloodline that far.

"Keeping aside the danger your children faced or are in danger to face, you should always remember the fact that it started with your generation and you were also involved in that night so after finishing the next generation the devil might be wanting to finish the present one." Exclaims Eve. "You are right that's why I was planning to send Laurene back to her mother's house in order to keep her safe, but then she denied as she told me that it's her fate of being with me in a relationship, and now she is ready to bear the consequences..." Jonathan recalled.

"I think after listening to this fairy like story I need some time to digest the truth or whatsoever it is, so I guess, I'll be leaving now" Brennan replies as he draws his footsteps closer to the main gate. "Wait! Don't think you'll be leaving this creature behind (as she points towards herself)". "If you want to go with me then hurry up because I've got some dinner plans this evening!" announces Brennan. "Is it a girl? Are you going on a date? Or can I say a blind date?" As Eve wanted to know. "Chill! You are being too far with that, it's just a school time friend, specially, a male friend so there's no need of panic, though why would you care?" inquired Brennan. "I've no problem I was just making sure you are not distracted by any girl during this case..." Eve says mockingly.

43

CHAPTER SIX

THE MIST WOODS

"Trust me! We as some normal investigators can't help the Holmes' in some supernatural work! We need any monk to help us out... can't we look for some ghost catchers online?" Asks Eve being impatient. "Come on we can't find any traditional man on internet, can't we ask Noah about that, I heard his village background is kind of mysterious and there had been monks living there since ages we can't even count on fingers!" he suggested. So, do we need to tell him about what happened today or what is happening from the past?" Eve asks. "I think it is the time to tell everyone about this including Sir Simpson!" advised Brennan. "Ok then, I don't think we should keep it a secret for any long..."

"You two are impossible to deal with, we are here dying to get any hint even if it's any smaller one, and you are casually walking with the biggest clue in your pant pockets from the past 1 week!" exclaimed Simpson. "Then, when would we'll be departing for my hometown? It's a little bit faraway place so we'll need to invest at least 4 hours if we go by air route and if we go by land route it's even longer..." informed Noah. "But according to our budget we can only afford going by land rout..." replies Brennan. "So, then it's decided that we'll be leaving tomorrow evening." Says Eve.

The Long Drive to Mist wood

As the investigation team set off early in the morning, the excitement was palpable. They had been driving for hours, watching the scenic countryside roll by outside their windows. To pass the time, they engaged in lively conversations.

"Did you guys notice anything weird about that village we're heading to?" Simpson asked, breaking the silence. "Weird? Like what?" Noah replied, raising an eyebrow. "I don't know, it just feels off. I've been researching, and there's hardly any information available online." "That's because it's a remote village," Noah explained. "Not many people venture there, so it's not surprising."

"I've heard rumors of mystical happenings in those parts," Eve chimed in. "Mystical? You mean supernatural?" Brennan's curiosity was piqued. "Exactly! People claim to have seen strange lights and heard whispers in the wind and in the mist woods." "That's fascinating!" Brennan exclaimed.

Just then, their driver interrupted, "We've got company!" He pointed to an old man with a long, flowing beard standing by the roadside, thumb raised. "Coincidence or fate?" Noah mused. The driver pulled over, and the old man climbed aboard. "Thank you, kind strangers. I'm headed to Mist wood Village." "The same place we're going!" Emily exclaimed. The old man's piercing gaze swept the group. "Ah, travelers seeking wisdom, I presume?"

"You could say that," Simpson replied cautiously.

"I am Ezra, a wanderer and seeker of truth. What draws you to Mist wood Village?" Ezra's eyes sparkled with curiosity.

Eve leaned forward. "We're investigating a series of bizarre occurrences. We heard a monk there might be able to help". "Mist wood Village holds secrets," Ezra whispered, "whispers of ancient rituals and forbidden knowledge." The team exchanged uneasy glances. As the hours passed, Ezra regaled them with tales of mysticism and wonder, weaving a spell of enchantment within the bus. "...and so, the villagers believe the forest whispers secrets to those who listen," Ezra concluded. "Whoa, that's deep," Brennan said, impressed.

The sun dipped below the horizon, casting a warm orange glow over the landscape. "We're approaching Mist woods Village," Noah announced. As they entered the village, an eerie silence enveloped them, punctuated only by the soft crunch of gravel beneath the tires. "Welcome to Mist woods Village," Ezra said, his voice low and mysterious. "May you find the answers you seek." With that, the bus came to a stop, and the team disembarked, stepping into the unknown.

As the team got separated with the monk, suddenly Brennan leaned into the woods spreading out his ears. "What are you up to now?" asks Noah miserably. "I'm trying to listen the secrets of the forest, maybe it whispers some of them in my ears too!" said Brennan, trying to poke at Noah and Ezra's beliefs.

As the team walked into the village, Noah led them to his family house, its emptiness echoing through the halls like a haunting lament. Eve's curious gaze met Noah's, and he knew she sought answers about his family. His voice cracked as he began to recount the tale of loss and longing that had ravaged his life.

"The whispers in the forest... they beckon those who've known sorrow, who've lost someone or something precious. My parents... they heard it too. It sounded like my younger brother's voice, calling out to them, tempting them with the

promise of reunion. He had passed away just days before, his fragile body succumbing to illness, leaving us shattered.

The whispers... they mesmerized my parents, drawing them in with a false hope. That fateful night, they slipped away, leaving me asleep, unaware of their departure. I awoke to an eerie silence, their absence a palpable weight crushing me. They never returned. The days turned into weeks, weeks into months, and months into years, but the ache remains, a gnawing sense of abandonment. I've scoured these woods, searched every glade, every stream, every shadow, but the truth eludes me.

Someone was there that night, a third presence lurking in the darkness, witnessing my parents' disappearance. I've spent years seeking that person, pleading for answers, but they remain elusive, leaving me with only tears and questions. My heart still holds onto the hope that they're out there, somewhere, waiting to be found. The whispers... they still echo through my mind, a haunting reminder of what I've lost, what I may never find". Noah's voice faltered, his eyes welling up with tears as the team's sympathetic gazes enveloped him. Eve consoled him but Brennan didn't want to admit he doesn't believe anything Noah just mentioned, but still had to agree for a while as he decided to think about it later.

Everyone was tired after having a small yet lovely dinner. "In this house I have 3 rooms only, two on the ground floor and one at the first floor. Brennan and Sir Simpson can share the one at the right corner and I'll take the one at the left corner, and Eve you can take the room on the first floor, I hope you have a good night spending here, tomorrow we'll be leaving to meet my family priest, I think this plan is okay with you all too..." announces Noah. After assuring everyone is comfortable with the stay Noah also went to his room.

The next day Noah took the team members to the house of their family priest. As Noah's fingers released the doorbell, he informed his team that he does not remember the name or even how he looks like as it has been years since he saw him last time in his parent's funeral. The team shared uneasy glances with each other. Finally, the door creaked open, revealing a bespectacled monk with an air of quiet contemplation. Noah immediately asked "Can we meet the master of this house, the great monk...?" "He's no longer here" the monk said, his voice barely above a whisper. "Our master abandoned this house, seeking solitude in the forest. Before departing, he instructed us to convert this residence into a sacred sanctuary and continue our spiritual pursuits."

Eve's curiosity go deepened as she asks "May we know his name?" The monk's response hung in the air like a challenge: "Ezra." The team's collective gasp was palpable, their minds reeling from the staggering coincidence. Just yesterday, they had given a ride to a mysterious stranger named Ezra, who had thanked them and vanished into thin air upon arrival in the village. The synchronicity was unnerving.

As they bid farewell to the monk and settled beneath a nearby tree, their hushed discussion was laced with incredulity. "What are the chances?" Eve whispers, her eyes wide with wonder. Noah's expression was grim: "This can't be a coincidence. There's something more to Ezra's story." Simpson's brow furrowed: "Think about it – we pick up a stranger, and he just happens to share the same name as the priest who's connected to Noah's family? This is either fate or a carefully crafted web of deceit." The team's unease deepened, their perception of reality beginning to blur. Who was Ezra, really? A chance encounter or a calculated player in a larger game? Were some of the questions to be answered.

CHAPTER SEVEN

In Search Of Expert

The group sat beneath the tree their faces etched with determination. "No way this is a coincidence," Brennan said, shaking his head. "Ezra's story runs deeper." "I know," Eve agreed. "We have to find him. Now."

Simpson nodded vigorously. "I'm with Eve. This mystery just got a whole lot more interesting." Noah's eyes burned with urgency. "I need answers. My parents... their disappearance... Ezra might hold the key."

"Okay, let's break this down," Brennan said, his analytical mind kicking in. "Ezra's connection to the priest, the whispers in the forest... there's a pattern here." "And the fact he disappeared after we dropped him off?" Simpson added. Eve's voice rose. "We need to track him down. Now."

As dusk descended upon the village, the group reluctantly retreated to Noah's house, their exhausted bodies craving rest. The day's events had unraveled like a tangled thread, leaving them with more questions than answers. The forest's secrets would have to wait until dawn.

Noah's return to his childhood home stirred up a maelstrom of emotions. Memories of his parents lingered in every corner, every creak of the wooden floorboards. His grief, once numbed by determination, now throbbed like an open wound. As night deepened, the clock struck midnight. Noah's eyelids drooped, but before sleep could claim him, a faint scratching echoed outside his window. He rose, his heart heavy, as he approached the pane.

A black cat perched on the sill, its emerald eyes glowing like lanterns in the darkness. Noah froze, transfixed by the hypnotic gaze. The cat's stare seemed to bore into his soul, awakening a primal connection. Ten seconds ticked by, and Noah's paralysis broke. He felt an inexplicable pull, as if the cat's eyes had awakened a deep-seated compulsion.

Without a word, Noah followed the cat out the window, into the darkness of the forest, the darkness of forest deepened as he slowly enters the new biome of mystery. Eve's slumber was shattered by a faint noise. She stirred, rubbed her eyes, and approached the window. The sight before her made her blood run cold. The black cat was going deep down into the forest, her eyes fixed on the cat. Eve trembled, fear clawing at her mind. How did it find them? The cat's presence seemed sinister, a harbinger of darkness. As she watched, Noah emerged from the shadows, his eyes vacant, his movements robotic. He followed the cat into the forest, disappearing into the blackness.

Eve's scream lodged in her throat. She spun around, racing to Brennan and Simpson's room. "Noah's gone!" she whispered urgently, shaking them awake. "He's following that... that cat!" Brennan's eyes snapped open. "What?"

Simpson bolted upright. "The cat from the road?" Eve nods, her face ashen. "It's here. Noah's gone after it." Without wasting another second the trio ran towards the forest. As they chased after Noah, the silence grew thicker, heavy with foreboding. Branches creaked, leaves rustled, and the cat's emerald eyes seemed to mock them, leading them deeper into the heart of terror. "What's happening?" Brennan panted as his voice barely audible. Simpson's face was set. "We don't know, but we can't lose Noah. "Eve's fear threatened to overwhelm her. "What if we're too late?"

The darkness swallowed their words, leaving only the sound of their frantic footsteps and the haunting feeling that they were being herded toward some ancient, malevolent force. The forest seemed to be waiting, its secrets coiled like a snake, ready to strike.

As they emerged into deep forest, forgetting the direction they came from they saw a house in the forest, there was only one single house surrounded by darkness and having two lanterns lighten up, hanging on the roof. There they saw the cat drinking milk from a bowl placed on the outer corner of the house and shoes of Noah lying in front of the entry gate, there was no doubt Noah was inside the house, the trio collected courage and began stepping towards the house as the low mewing echoed in their ears with the gesture of growling and mystery that lies in the house.

As they approached the foreboding house, its isolation and eerie silence sent shivers down their spines. The creaking of the trees and the rustling of leaves seemed to amplify their apprehension. Brennan's firm knocks on the door echoed through the stillness, and they exchanged uneasy glances. The door swung open, revealing Ezra's enigmatic smile.

"Welcome," he said, his eyes glinting with a knowing intensity. "Please, come in." Their hesitation was palpable, but Ezra's reassuring gesture beckoned them forward. As they stepped inside, they were met with an unsettling sense of familiarity. Noah sat calmly on the couch, his eyes vacant, his expression serene.

Ezra guided them to the dining room, the air thick with anticipation. "Please, take a seat," he said, his voice dripping with an air of mystery. The room was dimly lit, the shadows cast by the flickering candles dancing across Ezra's face. "I must confess," he began, his voice low and measured, "I orchestrated Noah's... invitation. Hypnosis, you see, can be a powerful tool. I needed you to follow him, to find this place."

Eve's eyes narrowed. "Why?" Ezra's smile widened. "Secrets, my friends. Secrets that have been hidden for far too long. This village, this forest... they hold mysteries beyond your wildest imagination." Brennan's skepticism was palpable. "What secrets?"

Ezra's gaze seemed to bore into their souls. "The whispers in the forest, the disappearances... it's all connected. And I'm willing to share it with you." Simpson's curiosity got the better of him. "What do you know about Noah's parents?"

Ezra's expression turned somber. "Ah, yes... the tragic loss. I know more than you think." Noah's vacant stare began to unsettle them. Was he still under Ezra's hypnosis? As they sat around the dining table, the atmosphere grew heavier, the silence punctuated only by the soft ticking of a clock. "What secrets, Ezra?" Eve pressed, her voice barely above a whisper. Ezra's eyes sparkled. "All will be revealed... in due time."

The room seemed to darken, as if the shadows themselves were closing in.

CHAPTER EIGHT

SHADOWS OF THE PAST

Ezra's eyes gleamed with an unnerving intensity as he began to weave a tale of darkness and despair. The room seemed to shrink, the shadows deepening, as if the very walls were listening.

"This village," Ezra started, his voice low and hypnotic, "has been shrouded in secrecy for centuries. Its history is stained with blood, tears, and the whispers of the damned." Brennan's skepticism faltered, replaced by a growing unease. Eve's eyes were wide, her face pale. Simpson's grip on his chair tightened.

"Noah's parents," Ezra continued, "were not the first to vanish. Many have disappeared, drawn by the whispers in the forest. Some sought answers, others solace. All were consumed." Noah's vacant stare remained the same as he can't seem to process the words uttered. His mind still trapped in Ezra's hypnotic grasp.

"The village's founders," Ezra revealed, "made a pact with an ancient power, trading innocence for protection. The forest became a conduit, a gateway to realms beyond our own." Eve's voice trembled. "What realms?" Ezra's smile was a thin, cruel line. "Realms of darkness, where the lost souls dwell. The whispers are their calls, beckoning the living to join them."

Simpson's face twisted in horror. "You mean... the village is cursed?" Ezra nodded. "Cursed, haunted, and bound to the will of the ancient power. The villagers live in ignorance, blinded by fear and superstition." Brennan's mind reeled. "And you, Ezra? What's your role in this?" Ezra's eyes flashed with a fierce light. "I'm the keeper of secrets, the guardian of the living. And I've been waiting for you, to share the burden of this knowledge." The room fell silent, the weight of Ezra's words crushing them.

Suddenly, Noah's eyes flickered, his gaze focusing on Ezra. "Wha... what happened to my parents?" he stammered, his voice shakingly. "Sorry I can't tell you anything about that this early..." replies Ezra. Ezra's expression softened, his voice gentle he added. "I'll show you, Noah. I'll show you everything." Noah's face contorted in anguish. "Tell me!" Ezra's smile returned, sinister and knowing. "All in due time, Noah. All in due time."

Eve's curiosity got the better of her. "The cat... how does it fit into all this?" Ezra's gaze drifted to the shadows, where the cat seemed to be watching. "She's the Guardian of Spirits. I feed her milk daily, pleading for the safety of the living. When I fail, she claims a life." Noah's eyes widened in horror. "My parents...?"

Ezra's expression turned somber. "I forgot to feed her that day. It happened because of me." Simpson's face darkened. "And Andrea? What happened to her?" Ezra's voice cracked. "I was late that day. The Guardian... they forgave me, but at a terrible cost. They dehumanized her, turned her into a demon."

Eve's mind racing, she asked, "If Andrea was attacked, it means she was somehow related to this forest?" Ezra nodded. "I've been searching for that connection. But I couldn't find anything." Brennan shared their discovery. "Andrea's father was a black magician, possibly connected to this forest."

Ezra's eyes snapped back to life. "But Andrea herself?"

Simpson added, "her father only learned magic from a book her brother found in a temple near the village. No blood ties to the local families." Ezra's face paled. "This change everything. We must find the connection between Andrea and the forest."

The room fell silent, the weight of their task settling in. Ezra's determination grew. "I'll share all my knowledge. Together, we'll uncover the truth." As they began their investigation, the shadows seemed to deepen, the forest's secrets waiting to be unraveled.

The next day Ezra guided them towards Noah's house. That day they decided to relax and explore the village and try to talk with some of them, they knew this was a difficult task as most of the people acted like introverts which never waved even a hello towards strangers and were busy in their own stuff. After wandering around the village for the whole day in evening Noah sent his team members to his house and bought some flowers and decorated them on the graves of his parents and his younger brother, he prayed for their peace in heaven, and after some time left for his home.

As night descended upon the village, Noah retreated to his bedroom, his heart heavy with the day's events. The comforting dinner and warm conversation with his friends couldn't shake off the lingering sorrow. He lay down, exhaustion claiming him.

Sleep enveloped him like a shroud, but his reprieve was short-lived. A presence invaded his dreams, its ethereal form twisting into grotesque shapes. Noah's subconscious recognized the spirit, its eyes burning with malevolent intent. "Your brother is not where you think," the spirit hissed, its voice like a rusty gate.

Trees loomed, their branches grasping like skeletal fingers. The spirit's taunts echoed through the darkness. "You worshipped like fools... Your brother can never find heaven." Noah's desperation grew, his dream-self stumbling through the underbrush. Suddenly, he stopped, defiance igniting within him. "My brother was good!" he shouted, his voice shaking. "He deserves heaven!"

The spirit's grin faltered, its expression contorting into grief.

"Ah, so sad... You, poor soul," it whispered, its voice dripping with malice. "Thinking your brother resides in a realm as peaceful as heaven... If you believe that, why don't you go and find your brother? Find the place you left him?" The spirit's words cut through Noah's resolve like a cold wind. His dream-self faltered, confusion replacing determination. Before he could respond, the spirit lunged, its presence crushing Noah's dreams. He jolted awake, sheets drenched in sweat, his heart racing.

Breathless, Noah sat up, the darkness of his room suffocating. The spirit's words lingered, echoing through his mind. Find the place you left him? What did it mean? Where had he left his brother? Memories of his brother's funeral flooded back, the pain and grief still raw. Noah threw off the covers, his resolve solidifying. He would uncover the truth, no matter the cost.

With shaking hands, he lit a candle, the flickering flame casting eerie shadows on the walls. Eve, Brennan, and

Simpson were already awake by the sounds of Noah shouting, their faces etched with concern. "Noah, what happened?" Eve asked, rushing to his side. Noah's voice trembled. "The spirit... It told me my brother isn't where I think." Brennan's eyes narrowed. "What does it mean?" Noah's determination grew. "I'll find out. I'll uncover the truth about my brother's disappearance."

Noah's sudden sprint left his friends stunned. "Noah, stop!" Eve cried, chasing after him. "Where are you going?" Brennan and Simpson flanked her, their faces etched with concern. Noah's determination only grew, fueled by the spirit's haunting words. He reached the graveyard, his brother's headstone looming before him. With a primal roar, he heaved the heavy rock covering the grave. "NOAH, STOP!" Simpson shouted, grasping for his arms.

Undeterred, Noah began scratching the soil with frenzied intensity. Eve and Brennan tried to restrain him, but he shook them off. "What are you doing, Noah?" Eve pleaded. Noah's response was a guttural growl, his eyes fixed on the dirt. Layer by layer, he uncovered the emptiness beneath.

Twenty minutes passed. The silence punctuated only by Noah's ragged breathing. Finally, his fingers closed around something metallic, A locket. The team's collective gasp echoed through the graveyard. Noah's brother was not there. No bones, no remains. Just the locket. Eve's voice trembled. "What... what does this mean?" Brennan's face paled. "Where's his body? And if it's rotten then where are his bones?"

Simpson's eyes scanned the surrounding area, as if expecting some monstrous entity to emerge. Noah's shaking intensified, his mind reeling from the implications. The spirit's words now made sense – his brother was never buried. With great effort, they coaxed Noah back to his house, his eyes vacant, his soul shattered.

Inside, Eve guided him to the couch, wrapping a blanket around his shivering frame. Brennan handed him a warm glass of water. "Drink, Noah," he urged softly. Noah's hands trembled, water spilling as he raised the glass to his lips.

Simpson's voice was barely audible. "We'll find out what happened, Noah. We promise." As Noah's eyelids drooped, Eve whispered, "Sleep, Noah. We'll be here." The room seemed to darken, shadows creeping in, as Noah's exhausted body succumbed to sleep. But his mind remained awake, tormented by the question: Where was his brother's body? And what had happened to it? The night wore on, the team's vigilant eyes fixed on Noah, their hearts heavy with foreboding. For in that moment, they knew they were entangled in a horror beyond imagination.

The next day, Noah's determination drove him to the attic, a dusty, forgotten realm. He scoured every trunk, every box, seeking answers. As he lifted the lid of an old chest, a yellowed envelope caught his eye. His heart skipped a beat. The letter, penned in his mother's handwriting, was addressed to him.

With trembling hands, Noah unfolded the paper.

"Dear Noah,

We don't know how much time we have now to spend with you, but we promise each and every second will be memorable we don't know how longer it lets us live, we have done some sins against the guardian of spirits, it never forgave us we even consulted it with Ezra, he was sorry that he cannot help us or make us have a long life, we were afraid about what would happen to you that's why we are preparing to end you somewhere far away from this horrible place so that the spirits don't follow you... but sadly if you are reading this then you came back to this place even when Ezra ordered you to not even look behind while going away. Now if you are here, we don't want you to be trapped by these spirits...

With love we wish you a future we couldn't give you, we hope you become a successful man in life, it's our misfortune that the god didn't want us to live happily with you...

Yours caring Louissa and Mario"

After reading the letter Noah's eyes were filled with water as the tears roll down his cheek, he quickly wiped them off and went out of the attic to have breakfast with his team.

CHAPTER NINE

FINDING THE FORGOTTEN

"You all should see it yourself if you don't believe me, I myself am holding the papers of adoption, it is clear that Asher wasn't born to Holmes but was brought to Holmes, he was adopted but he has no idea about this, the Holmes haven't told him yet, and they are requesting me to not disclose this in front of him too..." says the message an investigator sent them after the search ended at Holmes' house.

"That's interesting..." exclaims Simpson. "Maybe that's the reason he was not being attacked... because he does not belong to the family by blood!" wonders Eve. "Good thing that he'll be safe now!" sighs Brennan, as they finished their breakfast and thanked god for today's meal.

"So... from where should we start to find something about your brother's ending moments?" asks Brennan. "Shut up! We don't know if he's dead or alive, because we don't have his dead body buried in the grave!" announces Noah impatiently. "So... you said that Ezra was there in the funeral of your parents, what if he was also there on the funeral of your younger brother? Implies Brennan. "Could be possible!" exclaims Noah with a suggestion to go and meet Ezra. As they began to walk into the forest the mist covered them completely, they couldn't see the directions properly where they were supposed to go.

After an hour of wandering in the mist woods, they finally reached their destination it was a perfect time as they saw Ezra having some tea and sitting near the garden on his lawn chair.

"Noah, my boy," Ezra said, setting his cup aside. "What brings you here today?" Noah's voice trembled as he walked towards him. "Were you at my brother's funeral?" Ezra nodded. "Yes, I was there. I saw them lay your brother to rest." "No, you didn't!" Noah's face contorted in anguish. "You're lying! They weren't burying my brother, just his locket!" The group fell silent, the air thick with tension. Ezra's expression shifted from calm to shock.

"Oh... you've found out," Ezra whispered, his eyes darting between Noah and his friends. Noah's eyes blazed with anger and sorrow. "Tell us the truth, Ezra." Ezra's shoulders sagged, his voice barely above a whisper. "It's true... your brother was never buried." The words hung in the air like a challenge.

"It happened during the traditional carnival of Mist Woods," Ezra began, his voice measured. "Your parents took you to the carnival, leaving your younger brother behind. He was too sick to attend."

Noah's eyes widened, memories flooding back. "I was at my uncle's house that night," Noah said, his voice cracking.

Ezra nodded. "Yes, your parents left you there, thinking it would be a fun night for you. But when they returned home... your brother was gone." The group listened, entranced, as Ezra continued.

"I told your parents about the spirits of the forest. On carnival night, they choose a person, usually someone lonely, unwanted, or forgotten. Your brother was the chosen one."

Eve's hand flew to her mouth, horror etched on her face. "Why did they lie?" Brennan asked, his voice laced with empathy. Ezra's gaze dropped. "Your parents thought of your younger brother as a burden. They were ashamed, fearing ridicule from the village. So, they told everyone he died from illness." Noah's face crumpled, tears streaming down his cheeks. "My brother... wasn't loved?"

Ezra's expression softened. "That's not true, Noah. Your parents loved you both, but fear and shame consumed them." The group sat in stunned silence, the weight of Ezra's words crushing them.

Simpson spoke up, his voice gentle. "What happened to Noah's brother?" Ezra's eyes clouded. "The spirits took him. I don't know whether he is alive or is dead but, in my opinion, he might be dead by now." Noah's sobs echoed through the garden as his heart shattered by listening the truth about his parents.

Noah's determination fueled the group's resolve. "We need to uncover the truth," he said, his voice firm. Eve nodded. "What really happened to your brother?" Brennan shouldered his backpack. "Let's find out." Simpson's eyes sparkled with curiosity. "The spirits, the forest... there's more to this story."

Ezra's expression remained grave. "Be cautious. The truth may be more than you can handle." The group ventured into Mist Woods, seeking answers. As they delved deeper, the forest's silence enveloped them. "Noah, what if we don't find anything?" Eve asked. Noah's jaw clenched. "We will. We have to."

As they bid Ezra farewell and stepped away from his house, the darkness seemed to swallow them whole. The crunch of gravel beneath their feet echoed through the stillness. Suddenly, footsteps echoed from behind. They spun around to find Ezra's house plunged into darkness. The lights extinguished like a snuffed candle. "Noah, what's going on?" Eve whispered, her voice trembling. Before Noah could respond, a chill swept over them. Andrea stood near the milk pot, her eyes glowing with an otherworldly light. The black cat beside her seemed to growl, its fur bristling. With a twisted smile, Andrea tilted the pot, spilling milk across the ground.

The cat's eyes blazed with fury. It sprang to life, racing toward them with a blood-curdling screech. Panic set in as the team turned to flee. Brennan stumbled, his backpack snagging on a branch. Simpson yanked him free, and they sprinted through the forest. Trees blurred together, their branches grasping like skeletal fingers. The cat's snarls grew louder, closing in. Eve's breath came in ragged gasps. Noah's heart pounded in his chest.

Just as they thought they'd escape, the forest erupted in a deafening roar. The spirit of the forest loomed before them, its presence suffocating.

"LEAVE MIST WOODS!" it thundered. "NEVER RETURN!"

The team burst through the forest's edge, gasping for air. As they stumbled into the moonlit clearing, the spirit's voice faded into the distance. They didn't stop running until the trees were mere silhouettes. Breathless, they collapsed onto the grassy slope.

"What just happened?" Brennan stammered. Noah's eyes locked onto the forest. "We're not going back." But as they gazed into the darkness, a faint whisper seemed to carry on the wind: "You'll return... and I'll be waiting."

The morning sunlight struggled to penetrate the darkness lingering within them. Gathered around the breakfast table, the group hesitantly recounted the previous night's horrors. Eve shuddered, her voice barely above a whisper. "I never thought Andrea would follow us." Brennan's expression remained grim. "This is her domain now. We're the intruders." The group's anxiety was palpable, their resolve to never return to Mist Woods unwavering. But then, Simpson's eyes widened, and he slammed his fist on the table. "Wait! The milk was spilled!"

Eve's confusion mirrored the others. "What does that mean? Simpson's words tumbled out in a rush. "The cat didn't get its milk last night. That means... someone else did." Brennan's brow furrowed. "What are you saying?" Simpson's face paled. "Someone else was taken. Because of us, one of the villagers is gone."

The table fell silent, as if the air had been sucked out. Noah's mind reeled, his thoughts racing to Ezra. "Ezra," Noah whispered, his heart sinking. "We have to check if he's... alive." The group exchanged fearful glances. Without a word, they pushed back their chairs, abandoning their breakfast. The weight of their actions pressed upon them, propelling them toward the forest once more.

As they reluctantly entered the forest, the trees seemed to loom over them, their branches grasping like accusatory fingers. "Noah, what if..." Eve's voice trailed off. Noah's jaw clenched. "We have to know." Their footsteps quickened, driven by a growing sense of dread. Suddenly, Ezra's house came into view.

As they stepped into Ezra's tranquil garden, the tension dissipated, replaced by relief. Ezra sat serenely in his lawn chair, cradling a steaming cup of tea, his eyes closed, basking in the warm sunlight. The group approached with their footsteps quiet on the gravel path. Ezra's eyes opened, and a warm smile spread across his face.

"Ah, welcome back, my friends. Please, join me." He gestured to the empty chairs beside him.

They sat, still shaken but grateful for the peaceful atmosphere. Ezra continued, "Observe nature's beauty. The way the sunlight filters through the leaves, the gentle rustle of the breeze... it's mesmerizing." Noah's hands clenched into fists, unable to shake off the lingering unease. "Ezra, we need to talk." His voice disrupted the serene ambiance.

Ezra's expression turned inquiring. "What's troubling you, Noah?" Noah's words spilled out in a rush. "Last night... we saw Andrea, the black cat... the milk was spilled. Simpson thinks someone was taken." Ezra's teacup halted mid-air, his eyes widening in shock. "What?" He set the cup down, his hands trembling.

"We didn't want to come back," Eve added, "but we had to know if you're... safe." Ezra's face paled. "I'm fine, but... this changed everything." He rose from his chair, urgency etched on his face. "We must find the missing person. Immediately."

Brennan stood. "Do you know who it could be?" Ezra's eyes clouded. "I fear it may be someone close to us. We need to investigate, discreetly." Simpson's voice was laced with concern. "What if Andrea's still out there?" Ezra's jaw clenched. "We'll face her if necessary. But first, we must locate the missing person."

The group's determination solidified, forged in the fire of suspense and urgency. As they prepared to embark on their perilous quest, the silence was shattered by a faint whisper, carried on the wind: "Too late... the darkness has claimed another."

As dusk descended, the group reconvened, exhausted and defeated. Their search yielded nothing - no signs of disturbance, no missing person reports. The village seemed untouched, tranquil. Ezra's anxiety deepened. His eyes etched with worry.

"We need to check the temple," he urged, leading them toward the ancient structure. The temple's entrance, once a beacon of solace, now loomed ominously. Ezra's gaze swept the empty stairs, his face crumpling. "He's gone," he whispered, his voice trembling.

"Who?" Noah asked, confusion etched on his face "The beggar," Ezra replied, his eyes welling up. "He always sat here, on these stairs. I'd talk with him for hours... He'd share his stories, his struggles." Eve's hand instinctively reached out, offering comfort. "Why was he safe for so long?"

Ezra's voice cracked. "I... I worshipped for his safety every time I left milk outside my house. He'd beg me to protect him from the spirits. Hc'd say, 'Ezra, I've lived a life of misery, but don't let them take me.' I promised him... I promised."

Brennan's eyes narrowed. "When did you last see him?"

Ezra's gaze drifted into the past. "Two years ago, when I left my old home. But... I saw him again the day I traveled with you all to this village. He was sitting here, on these stairs... smiling."

Simpson's voice was barely audible. "Do you think Andrea took him?" Ezra's face contorted in anguish. "I should have protected him. I failed."

CHAPTER TEN

Departure And Doubt

As the sun dipped below the village's horizon, Noah, Eve, Simpson, Brennan, and Ezra stood outside the temple, discussing their next move. Ezra's expression remained stoic, but a hint of determination flickered in his eyes. "I'll keep digging here, see if I can uncover any leads on the beggar's disappearance." Noah nodded. "We'll investigate every angle in the city. Simpson, we need you to head back with us. Your expertise is crucial."

Simpson's phone buzzed, and he answered, listening intently. "Understood, Director. We're on our way." He turned to the group. "Headquarters needs us. There's been a breakthrough in the case." Eve's eyes narrowed. "What kind of breakthrough?" Simpson's expression turned serious. "The director didn't specify, but we're required to report immediately." Brennan's jaw set.

"Looks like our work here is done. Let's get back to the city." With swift farewells, Ezra remained in the village, while the team departed. They were confused with their sudden departure as they didn't have the time to pack all the stuff some still wondered if they left something.

As the team departed the village, Brennan suddenly spoke up. "Who ate the last of the energy bars?" Eve rolled her eyes. "You know it was you, Brennan." Simpson chuckled. "Energy bars are your love language, Brennan."

Noah smiled. "Focus, team. We have a case to crack." Brennan grinned. "Right, right. The case. I'm just fueling my detective skills." Eve teased, "With all the energy bars?" The team's banter continued until they arrived at headquarters. Director Rachel greeted them, her expression serious. "Welcome back, team. We've received an anonymous tip. A witness claims to have seen Andrea near an abandoned warehouse."

Noah's eyes narrowed. "What's the witness's credibility?" Director Rachel replied, "Unverified, but the description matches Andrea's profile." Simpson asked, "What's the plan?" Director Rachel said, "Assemble your gear. You leave in one hour." Brennan whispered to Eve, "Time to gear up... and find more energy bars." As Eve playfully hit him on the arm, they walked out of the office.

The team arrived at the abandoned warehouse, their flashlights casting eerie shadows on the walls. "Alright, let's move in," Simpson directed, his voice firm. "Noah, take point. Brennan, cover our six. Eve, we'll need you to analyze any evidence we collect, but please remain outside, secure the perimeter."

Eve nodded, setting up her mobile lab near the entrance. Noah led the way, his eyes scanning the dimly lit warehouse. "Clear," he whispered. Brennan covered the rear, his gun drawn. "All clear." Simpson examined the entrance. "No signs of forced entry. Brennan, what do you make of this?"

Brennan holstered his gun. "Looks like our witness might've been telling the truth. This place hasn't been used in years." As they combed the warehouse, Simpson spotted a faint symbol etched into the wall, resembling the village's temple inscriptions.

"Noah, take a closer look," Simpson ordered. "Brennan, get some photos." Noah examined the symbol. "Looks similar to the village's markings." Brennan snapped photos. "This could be our connection. "Suddenly, a faint noise echoed through the house. Simpson's voice was calm. "Hold positions. Noah, check it out."

"Guys, I've got something!" Simpson called out. Noah and Brennan rushed to his side. Inside the compartment lay A cryptic note: "Echo-12: Andrea's legacy" and a USB drive. Brennan's eyes narrowed. "What's Echo-12?" Simpson inserted the USB drive into his phone. "Let's see what's on this." The screen flickered to life, revealing: A video of Andrea, speaking directly to the camera.

As the team watched the video, Andrea's eerie smile sent chills down their spines. Her voice dripped with sadistic pleasure.

"Let's play a game at my house tonight... Hide and seek. You all would hide, and I'll find you. Imagine how fun this can be..." Andrea's eyes glinted with malevolence. "But if you're late for the game, you'll be punished..." The camera zoomed in on Andrea's face, her pupils dilating.

"I've prepared a special surprise for you. My house has many secrets, many hiding spots. You'll never find them all." Andrea's voice dropped to a whisper. "But I will find you. I always do."

Noah's face paled. "What have we gotten ourselves into?" Brennan's jaw clenched. "This isn't just a game. It's a trap." Simpson's eyes narrowed. "We need to get to Holmes' house tonight, ASAP." The video continued, Andrea's words dripping with malice.

"You'll hide, but I'll be watching. I'll be waiting. And when I find you... " Andrea's smile grew wider. "You'll wish you never played this game."

Suddenly, the camera flickered, and Andrea's face distorted. "Come and play... Come and play..." The words echoed, growing louder, more menacing. Eve's voice trembled. "Turn it off. Please." But Simpson's gaze remained fixed on the screen. The camera zoomed out, revealing Andrea's surroundings. A dimly lit hallway, cobwebs clinging to the walls.

It was 4 in the evening Brennan was sitting against Eve drinking coffee while thinking about the chain of incidents happening with them lately. "May I have the bill please" asks Eve as today was her turn to pay. "Don't forget that we have to reach at Holmes today at 6 PM I don't want to be late for the free drama show!" exclaims Brennan teasing the fact that today only they received one dramatically horror invitation through video.

Eve and Brennan waitcd anxiously outside Holmes' mansion, their concern growing as Simpson and Noah failed to arrive on time. Andrea's sinister game was set to begin at 6:00 PM, and they were already running perilously late. "Six-ten already, and they're still not here," Eve said, her voice laced with worry. "We're supposed to be inside, preparing, but now we're four minutes late, and Andrea's so-called game has likely started without us."

Just then, Simpson's car pulled up, and he stepped out, accompanied by Noah, explaining, "Sorry we're late; traffic on Main Street was terrible, and it took us longer than expected." Brennan's frustration boiled over. "We're late because of you two! And we're walking into the unknown, unprepared."

Simpson's expression turned grim. "Let's move, now. We can't waste another minute."

CHAPTER ELEVEN

THE ILL-FATED MATE

As they entered the mansion, the group was met with an unsettling sight: Jonathan, Andrea's father, slumped in a corner, his body racked with sobs. They rushed to his side, concern etched on their faces. "Brennan, Eve, thank God you're here," Jonathan stammered, his eyes red-rimmed. "I...I don't know what happened. My wife, Laurenc...she was taken from me."

Simpson's voice was firm but gentle. "What do you mean 'taken'? Who took her?"

Jonathan's face contorted in anguish. "Andrea...our daughter. She was supposed to be...gone. But she appeared in the kitchen, asking for a bite of food. Laurene and I were cooking together...and then...Andrea's eyes...they were...different. Eve's voice trembled. "What did Laurene say to Andrea?"

Jonathan's voice cracked. "Laurene told Andrea, 'No, you can't have any. You're not our daughter.' And then...Andrea...she just...took Laurene. Through the balcony window. It happened so fast...I couldn't even react." Noah's eyes widened. "What do you mean 'took'

Laurene?" Jonathan's words spilled out in a desperate rush. "Andrea grabbed Laurene and vanished. I ran to the window, but...there was nothing. No one. Just...empty space. I couldn't even scream. My voice was frozen in my throat."

Brennan's face set in determination. "We'll find Laurene. We'll get to the bottom of this."

Simpson's gaze locked onto Jonathan's. "Tell us everything, Jonathan. Every detail. What did Andrea say exactly?"

Jonathan's eyes welled up with tears. "She said... 'Can I have a bite too, Mommy?' Her voice was...so innocent. But her eyes...they were...evil. And Laurene...she just...pushed her away. Said those terrible words... 'You're not our daughter.' "Eve's voice was barely above a whisper. "And then Andrea took Laurene?"

Jonathan nodded, his body shaking. "Yes...in an instant. I'm telling you it was...supernatural. Andrea's not human. She's...something else." The group exchanged weighted glances, their minds racing with the implications. Suddenly, a faint sinister whisper seemed to echo through the room: "You were late so I chose my mate!!!"

"Wait what? We were late so she chose her mate?" trembled Eve while looking into Brennan's eyes as he assumed "Is she talking about Mrs. Holmes as her mate?". "It can be possible but why did she take her and what is she up to with that mate type of thing?" asks Simpson. "Hey! Are you in senses right now? We are just 10 minutes late!" shouts Noah breaking the weird silence in the room

"What should we do now... make a missing report? Or start the search mission?" Brennan asked as there was no other option for them to opt. "Are you seriously joking right now? My wife is missing and we all know it very well who took her... So, it's better to keep those formalities aside for a moment and just think about how you can find her!" shouts Jonathan pouring out his emotions.

"I can completely understand you sir but at this moment we are cops not your relatives who can just sit and gossip about the incidents while trying to find her and getting nothing in hand, we know how you feel right now but we can't just start anything or any mission just by listening your side... it would be done after some necessary official work." Informs Simpson. "Common team! We have a lot of work in line lets complete that first..." added Simpson giving a side eye to Jonathan.

"So... where should we start from? It's not like we are carrying some clues so we have to find her with just one belief- that Andrea took her?" asks Noah after reaching their headquarters. "Let me breath for a moment it's been days since we last came here!" announces Brennan while leaning his back into the chair. "Wait! We'll start from the beginning counting all the milestones we have reached in this case till now!" announce Simpson as he asked others some questions one by one- "So what do we know about Andrea?" he asks turning towards Eve. "We know that she is not like us anymore but something dangerous and can regenerate her limbs once detached..." Eve answers in a single breath. "And... any clues about her recent position?" asks Simpson staring at Brennan with cold sleepy eyes.

"I will find the answer as soon as my junior officer gives me some details about the nearby CCTV cameras." Informs Brennan as he picked up his phone and excused himself stepping out from the room. "Okay so, Noah you will come with me to visit miss Clara Vincent as she might be knowing something about Andrea, she was her closest friend after all..." Simpson informs Noah.

"Having someone by your side always is a blessing but we don't know for how long we will be delighted with that gift of god, sometimes it's hard to forget and that's why I myself was not able to attend my classes for days, all I did was simply sitting before the pictures we took together and crying while remembering those sweet memories I made with her... although we were together for only a few days but still she got a special place in my life so soon! Things went differently when she met Mike, all she talked about was Mike and I low key didn't like the way she was ruining our time together only talking about Mike. As she was new in this place my classmate spread rumors that on that evening, she might have lost her way and met her fate shortly after not getting enough food... I didn't believe that because somehow, I think if Mike didn't saw something then he really didn't saw something he is not a boy who likely tells lies. The only thing I felt was wrong was sending Mike to Juvenile before listening or understanding him..." claims Clara Vincent as they began their interview.

"Although we know Mike was telling the truth but we realized it sometime after he was sentenced in Juvenile. We'll try our best getting him out of there" adds Simpson comforting Clara about her claims. "So... can you give us some more details about Andrea Holmes as no one can know her better than you, we also didn't get any information about her previous school friends." Adds Noah as he finished with a sigh of tension.

"She was a bright student if I start with the perspective of our school teachers. In my opinion no one was as dumb as her!" as Clara chuckles with emotions brewing up into her eyes. I don't think I can provide you more details being just a classmate of hers, the case is serious and I don't want you to waste your time asking about Andrea to a dumb nerd like me…" as she continues. "We don't feel anything weird about interviewing any high school girl if it's important for our case… anyways we took a lot of time of yours, I guess, now we'll be leaving for this moment and I hope if we wish to investigate this further then you would be helping us with the case" informs Simpson as he concluded their meeting and walked out of her house.

As they walked past her street, they parted their ways as Noah was headed towards his house and Simpson had to visit the headquarters for submitting the reports of their investigation with Miss Clara Vincent. The next day was Sunday so they all had a day off which was a rare day as they barely get days off from office (even if it was one).

"So… what are your plans this Sunday? Are you going out? If not please meet me at our regular café I have something to discuss urgently" Eve typed the message and put her phone away as she leaned back into her chair while thinking about the schedule meeting she had tomorrow, it was surprisingly weird as tomorrow Noah and Brennan were told to visit the Lewin family.

The thing which was even more disturbing was that even Mike was ordered to come into the investigation, he is only a high school boy and in the views of Eve a child like him shouldn't be involved in such cases.

After some time, they both met at the café, had a seat and ordered their regular drinks. "So, what do you think about the meeting you are having tomorrow?" asks Eve without wasting much time. "I don't feel anything weird but I've heard from the nurses that since Mike came there, he's not been speaking likely. They feel he may be in trauma or something like that" informs Brennan as he pulled out his phone out of his pocket and excused himself.

"Okay... so he's not been speaking well enough, it can be possible as no one likes to be alone and away from home, but why is sir Simpson not going with them?" Eve talks to herself as she received her regular coffee.

CHAPTER TWELVE

CAN HE SPEAK NOW?

"Now it has been almost 6 weeks since Andrea was missing, and almost 6 weeks my son being apart from his family for no reason given till date! I am sorry to say but I might not be able to attend the family gathering this year… I hope you all will understand my situation right now. Today two members of the investigation team are going to visit my son so he'll be transferred from the juvenile, I'm so happy that today I'll get the chance to see my boy… it's been days since we last contacted each other I hope everything goes fine and soon my son gets out of that horrible place at once!"

As Mr. Lewin hung up the phone call from his cousin brother, he grabbed his coffee and sat beside the window watching the snowfall which reminded him some sweet memories from his son being with him whenever it snowed. He missed him so much that he couldn't wait to finally meet him! Controlling his emotions while holding back his tears maybe wouldn't work when he will meet his boy. It was always pleasing to have someone by your side but Mike was stuck in a situation where he had 'no one' by his side as he never uttered a word after he was sentenced punishment, maybe it was his mental trauma or his unwillingness to speak.

As the time passed it was 4 in the evening, the time when Jenipher would be finally meeting Mike after a long time he was scared and excited at the same time.

As Brennan and Noah arrived at Mike Lewin's residence, a sense of unease settled over them. The juvenile center had released Mike into his parents' care, citing concerns about his erratic behavior. The nurse, Mrs. Jenkins, greeted them with a worried expression. "Be gentle with him, detectives. He's been...different since his admission." She led them to Mike's room, where the once-cocky teenager now lay listlessly in bed.

"Can he speak now?" Brennan asked, his eyes scanning Mike's vacant expression. Mrs. Jenkins hesitated. "Honestly, he hasn't been sleeping or speaking properly since his admission. We think he's depressed about something, but he won't open up." Noah's brow furrowed. "Has he mentioned Andrea or the Holmes family?" Mrs. Jenkins shook her head. "No, nothing. Just random, nonsensical phrases." Brennan approached Mike's bedside, his voice firm but gentle. "Mike, we need to talk about Andrea. What do you know about her disappearance?"

Mike's gaze drifted, his eyes un focusing. "Cats...have...four legs..." Noah sighed. "Mike, focus. What happened with Andrea?" Mike's response was a whisper. "The sky is...blue...sometimes." Brennan tried again. "Did Andrea threaten you? Did she say something that scared you?" Mike's voice rose, his words tumbling out in a frantic stream. "Pineapples on pizza...wrong...just wrong...can't trust...the mailman..." The detectives exchanged frustrated glances. Mike's answers were gibberish, offering no insight into Andrea's case.

Suddenly, Mike's eyes locked onto Brennan's, a fleeting glimmer of lucidity. "Run...away...while you still can..." The moment passed, and Mike's gaze drifted off once more. Noah's voice was low. "What's he hiding, Brennan?" Brennan's jaw clenched. "We need to push him harder. There's something he's not telling us."

As they continued questioning Mike, the silence between his nonsensical responses seemed to grow thicker.

After an eternity of silence, Mike's voice cracked, and he whispered, "I have nightmares...about Andrea...every day." As Brennan's eyes locked onto Mike's, encouraging him to continue. "What kind of nightmares, Mike?" Noah asked, his tone softening.

Mike's eyes drooped, his voice barely audible. "She's always chasing me...laughing...her eyes are black...like coal." He shuddered, the memory visibly shaking him. "I try to run, but my legs won't move. She catches me, and...and..." Mike's voice faltered. Brennan's expression remained calm, but his eyes betrayed concern. "What happens when she catches you, Mike?"

Mike's whisper sent chills down their spines. "She whispers... 'You'll never escape...you'll play my game forever.'" Noah's grip on his notebook tightened. "Does she say anything else?" Brennan pressed. Mike's eyes welled up with tears. "Sometimes...she says... 'You should have helped me...now you'll never find Laurene.'" The detectives exchanged weighted glances; Laurene's disappearance was more connected to Andrea's game than they thought.

Noah's voice was gentle. "Mike, we're here to help. Tell us what really happened with Andrea." Mike's gaze pleaded for understanding. "I didn't know what she was capable of...I didn't know she'd take Laurene. I swear, I didn't know." As Brennan's expression remained unreadable.

"We'll uncover the truth, Mike. But you need to tell us everything."

As Mike's words spilled out, the shadows in the room seemed to deepen, as if Andrea's presence loomed, listening to their conversation. Brennan and Noah stepped out of the Lewin's house, the crisp evening air a stark contrast to the oppressive atmosphere inside. "I don't buy it," Brennan said, his voice low and tense. "What?" Noah asked, his eyes scanning the darkening street. "Mike's story. He's hiding something." Noah's expression turned thoughtful. "I agree. But what's he hiding?" Brennan's jaw clenched. "He knows more about Andrea's game than he's letting on." Noah's voice rose. "But what's the game? What's the end goal?" Brennan's eyes narrowed. "That's what we need to find out. Laurene's disappearance is just the beginning."

Noah's face set in determination. "We need to dig deeper into Mike's alibi. See if anyone can corroborate his story." Brennan nodded. "Andrea has got something on him. Something big." Noah's voice dropped to a whisper. "You think Mike's in danger?" Brennan's expression turned grim. "I think we all are." As they stood there, the shadows seemed to lengthen, casting long, ominous silhouettes across the pavement. Suddenly, Noah's phone buzzed. He glanced at the screen, his face pale.

"What is it?" Brennan asked. Noah's voice trembled. "It's an unknown number...text message... 'You're getting close. Back off now.'" Brennan's eyes locked onto Noah's. "Andrea's watching us." Brennan's eyes narrowed. "Get Simpson to track the number. I want to know who sent this."

Noah nodded, already dialing Simpson's number. "Simpson, we need you to track a number...unknown caller...sent a threatening text." Simpson's voice crackled through the phone. "Send me the message and the number. I'll get to work." Noah relayed the information, then turned to Brennan. "Simpson is on it."

Brennan's gaze scanned the surrounding area, his mind racing. "This changes the situations. Andrea's getting desperate." As Noah's expression turned grim. "We're getting close to something."

Simpson's voice came through the phone again. "Guys, I've got something. The number's registered to a burner phone, but I managed to triangulate the location." As Brennan's eyes locked onto Noah's. "Where?" Simpson's pause was palpable. "The Holmes' mansion." The darkness seemed to close in around them.

Brennan and Noah arrived at the Holmes' mansion, where they found Jonathan pacing anxiously in the foyer. "What's going on?" he asked, his eyes wide with concern.

"We've tracked a suspicious text message to this location," Brennan explained. "Can you tell us if anyone's been using a burner phone in the house?" Jonathan's expression turned puzzled. "I don't know...I haven't seen anything." As Noah's gaze locked onto Jonathan's. "We need to search the house. Now."

Jonathan hesitated before nodding. "Okay...let's start with Andrea's room." As they ascended the stairs, Simpson and Eve joined the group, their faces set with determination. Jonathan led them to Andrea's room, his hand trembling as he opened the door. Inside, the team found the burner phone on the bedside table, its screen dark. Brennan's gloved hand picked it up, examining it carefully. "No signs of recent use," he muttered.

Eve's voice was barely audible. "But how's this possible? Andrea's phone was locked in here since her disappearance." As Jonathan's eyes welled up with tears. "I...I don't understand. I thought she was gone." Noah's eyes narrowed. "Did you notice anything unusual, Mr. Holmes?" as Jonathan's voice cracked. "I...I heard noises at night. Creaks and groans. I thought it was just the house settling." as Brennan's expression turned grim. "We'll review the security footage. See if anyone's been in this room." Suddenly, Eve spotted a note on the bedside table. "Look."

The note, in Andrea's handwriting, sent chills down their spines: "You'll never find me. But I'll always find you." Jonathan's face contorted in anguish. "What does it mean?" as Brennan's voice was firm. "We'll find out, Mr. Holmes. We'll search every inch of this mansion."

The team huddled around the security room's screen their eyes fixed on the grainy footage. Brennan's voice was low and urgent. "Fast-forward to the time stamp when the burner phone sent the text." Simpson's fingers flew across the keyboard, and the footage blurred before snapping into focus. Andrea's figure appeared on screen, climbing through her bedroom window with an unnatural ease. Her face was twisted into a macabre grin, sending shivers down their spines. "Oh God..." Eve whispered, her hand covering her mouth. Noah's eyes widened. "How did she...?" Jonathan's face paled, his eyes welling up with tears. "My daughter...what's happened to you?"

The footage showed Andrea moving swiftly through her room, her movements almost ethereal. Five minutes passed, and then she reappeared at the window, slipping out into the darkness as silently as a ghost. Brennan's voice was grim. "Let's check the window."

As they approached Andrea's room, an unsettling feeling settled over them. The window was closed, its panes gleaming in the faint moonlight. Simpson examined the frame, his face puzzled. "No signs of forced entry or exit. No fingerprints."

Eve's voice trembled. "As if she never left." Noah's eyes scanned the room, his gun drawn. "Clear." As Brennan's gaze locked onto the window, his expression unyielding. "We need to dust for prints again. Check for any DNA evidence."

Jonathan's voice cracked. "What...what is she?" The room seemed to darken, as if Andrea's presence still lingered, watching them. Suddenly, a faint creak echoed through the hallway, making everyone's heart skip a beat.

"What was that?" Eve whispered. Noah's gun snapped up, his eyes scanning the shadows. Brennan's voice was low and deadly. "Let's move. Now." The team backed away from the window, their movements slow and deliberate, as if retreating from an unseen terror.

As the night wore on, the team reluctantly decided to call it a day, their minds reeling with questions and fears. "Let's reconvene at 8 AM," Brennan said, his eyes scanning the exhausted faces. Noah nodded. "I'll review the security footage again, see if I missed anything." Eve's voice was barely above a whisper. "I'll research possible connections to similar cases." Simpson yawned. "I'll dig deeper into Andrea's online activity." Jonathan's eyes, sunken and haunted, lingered on the team. "Find my daughter...please."

With somber nods, they departed the mansion, leaving Jonathan to his anguish. The darkness outside seemed to swallow them whole, each member lost in their own thoughts as they drove away. Brennan's eyes met his rearview mirror, the mansion's facade fading into the distance. A shiver ran down his spine.

"Noah, you still with me?" Brennan asked over the phone. "Yeah, just pulling into my driveway," Noah replied.

"You?" "Almost home. Keep your eyes open tonight." "You too."

The silence that followed was oppressive, each man lost in his own fears. Eve pulled into her apartment complex, her heart racing as she glanced around the deserted parking lot.

Simpson settled into his couch, his laptop open, but his mind elsewhere. As they settled in for the night, the shadows outside their windows seemed to grow longer, darker. Andrea's presence lingered, watching, waiting.

Noah pulled into his driveway, his eyes scanning the darkened neighborhood. The porch light cast an inviting glow. He stepped out of the car, feeling the weight of the day's events. The creak of the door, the familiar scent of his home, offered a sense of comfort. As he locked the door behind him, Noah's gaze fell on the photo of his brother, Lucas, who had gone missing years ago. The pain still lingered, and finding Andrea had become a personal crusade. Noah poured himself a glass of water, his mind replaying the security footage. Andrea's ethereal movements haunted him.

Suddenly, his phone buzzed. "Noah, it's Brennan. Just got a suspicious call. 'You'll never find her.'" Brennan's voice was low and urgent. Noah's grip on the phone tightened. "Think it's Andrea?" "Unknown number. But the voice...it was barely audible. Sent chills down my spine." Noah's eyes scanned his darkening living room. "I'll come over." "No, get some rest. We'll regroup at 8 AM." Noah nodded, though Brennan couldn't see him. "Stay vigilant." The line went dead.

CHAPTER THIRTEEN

NIGHT TERRORS

Mike woke up, feeling thirsty and disoriented. The medication had left him groggy, and his head spun as he swung his legs over the side of the bed. He rubbed his eyes, trying to shake off the haze.

As he shuffled downstairs, the cold night air clung to his skin, making him shiver. He flipped on the kitchen light, and the fluorescent glow illuminated the empty water jar. Mike let out a frustrated sigh. Just as he turned to grab a glass from the cabinet, he heard a whisper. The soft voice sent shivers down his spine. "Want a glass of water, Mike?" Mike's heart skipped a beat. He spun around, his eyes scanning the room. Andrea sat at the dining table, a toy car and a glass of water in front of her. Her smile was playful, pretty, and utterly unsettling.

For a moment, Mike forgot to breathe. Andrea looked... normal. The same sparkling eyes, the same golden complexion he remembered from school.

"Hey," Mike managed, his voice barely above a whisper. Andrea's smile grew wider. She picked up the toy car and began to play, her fingers moving with an unnerving delicacy. Mike's fear warred with fascination. What was she doing here? Why was she acting like this?

Andrea drowned the toy car in the water, her eyes glinting with mischief. "Oops! It's gone!" She chuckled, the sound sending shivers down Mike's spine. Mike's smile faltered. Something was off. Andrea's laughter seemed to be forced her smile too wide.

As he watched, Andrea's expression shifted. Her smile twisted, her skin pale and almost translucent. Her eyes darkened, like two voids sucking in the light.

Mike's heart racing, he took a step back. "Andrea?" Her voice dropped to a whisper, sending chills down his spine. "You shouldn't have looked for me, Mike." The air seemed to thicken, heavy with malevolence. Mike's vision blurred, and he felt himself being pulled toward Andrea. Suddenly, her face contorted, her skin turning a sickly pale blue. Her eyes bulged, and her smile grew grotesque. Mike's scream was trapped in his throat.

Andrea's voice grew louder, a cacophony of whispers. "You'll never find me. But I'll always find you." The room began to spin. Mike stumbled backward, his legs buckling. As he fell, Andrea's laughter echoed through the kitchen.

When Mike came to, he was lying on the kitchen floor, his head throbbing. The room was silent, except for the ticking clock. Andrea sat beside him, her creepy smile inches from his face. Her eyes gleamed with an otherworldly intensity.

"You're mine now, Mike," she whispered, her breath cold against his skin. Mike's heart racing, he tried to scramble away, but Andrea's icy grip held him in place.

Mike's vision blurred as Andrea's smile grew wider. Her hand closed around the knife, its blade glinting in the dim light. The air thickened with malevolence. Andrea's voice dripped with malice. "You'll never escape me, Mike." With a swift, merciless motion, Andrea plunged the knife into

Mike's belly. The blade sliced through flesh and muscle, twisting and turning, seeking out nerve endings. Mike's scream echoed through the kitchen, a sound of raw agony.

The pain exploded like a wild fire consuming Mike's senses. His vision blurred, and his body arched in a futile attempt to escape the torment. Andrea's grip on the knife tightened, her eyes flashing with sadistic pleasure. She twisted the blade, probing deeper, seeking the most sensitive nerves.

Mike's screams grew hoarse, his voice shredded by the relentless agony. His mind reeled, unable to comprehend the sheer intensity of the pain. Andrea's whisper sent shivers down Mike's spine. "You'll never find peace." With a slow, deliberate motion, Andrea withdrew the knife from Mike's belly. The blade slid out, leaving behind a trail of blood and shattered tissue.

Mike's respite was short-lived. Andrea's gaze locked onto his neck, her eyes gleaming with sinister intent. The knife descended, its point pressing against Mike's skin. Andrea's hand trembled with anticipation. Mike's eyes widened in terror as the blade sank deeper, millimeter by agonizing millimeter. His screams grew louder, a cacophony of despair.

The pain became a living entity, writhing inside Mike's mind like a serpent. His vision darkened, and his world narrowed to a single, horrific reality. Just as the darkness closed in, Mike jolted awake, gasping for air. His sheets were drenched in sweat, his heart racing.

Relief washed over him, followed by a creeping sense of unease. The pain lingered, a ghostly echo of the nightmare. Mike's hands trembled as he touched his belly, half-expecting to find the wound. But his skin was intact, unmarred. The memory of Andrea's twisted smile lingered, haunting him. Was it just a dream or a warning?

Mike's gaze fell on the window, where the darkness outside seemed to press in, eager to reclaim him.

Mike's ragged breathing slowed as he tried to shake off the lingering fear. His mind replayed the nightmare, Andrea's twisted smile etched into his memory. He threw off the covers and swung his legs over the side of the bed, wincing as his feet touched the cold floor. The room spun, and Mike gripped the bedframe to steady himself. In the bathroom, Mike splashed water on his face, trying to wash away the remnants of the nightmare. His reflection stared back, pale and haunted.

As he dried his face, Mike noticed something odd. A small, crimson droplet on his shirt. He touched the stain, and his heart skipped a beat. How did that get there? Mike's mind reeled. Was the nightmare more than just a dream? He stumbled back to bed, his thoughts racing. The pain from the dream still lingered, a dull ache in his belly. Mike's phone buzzed, shrill in the silence. A text from Noah: "Meet me at the café at 10. We need to talk." Mike hesitated, unsure if he was ready to face the world. But Noah's urgency was contagious.

As he dressed, Mike couldn't shake off the feeling that Andrea's presence still lingered, watching him from the shadows. After sometime he left his house without informing Mr. Lewin but he left a post it on the refrigerator in case his father would wake up and become tensed not finding him in his room.

At the café, Noah's expression was grim. "Mike, I've been researching Andrea's disappearance. I think I found something." Mike's heart sank. "What is it?" Noah leaned in, his voice barely above a whisper. "Andrea's not the only one who's gone missing. There are others, but all were with different locations the one common thing between these cases is that all the girls went missing strangely like this... they just disappeared."

Mike's grip on his coffee tightened. "What does it mean?" Noah's eyes locked onto Mike's. "I think Andrea's not just a victim. She's a key to something much darker."

Noah's concern etched on his face as he leaned in. "Mike, you look like you've seen a ghost. What's wrong?" Mike's eyes drifted, his voice barely above a whisper. "I had a dream...it felt so real." Noah's grip on his coffee tightened. "What happened in the dream?"

Mike's gaze locked onto Noah's, his words spilling out in a rush. "Andrea was in my kitchen. She had a toy car and a glass of water. She...she hurt me, Noah. The pain was unbearable." Noah's expression darkened. "What kind of pain?" Mike's face contorted, reliving the memory. "She stabbed me with a knife. I felt my skin tear, my nerves burning. It was like my body was on fire."

Noah's eyes narrowed. "And then?" Mike's voice dropped to a whisper. "I woke up. But the pain lingered. And when I came downstairs...the glass with the toy car was on the dining table. Exactly as I saw it in my dream." Noah's eyes widened. "That's impossible." Mike's eyes searched Noah's. "Is it? Or is something more sinister at play?" The café's background noise faded into the silence between them. Noah's mind raced with the implications.

Noah dialed Eve's number, hoping her forensic expertise could shed light on the mysterious glass and toy car. Twenty minutes passed, and Eve burst into the café, her blonde hair standing out amidst the drab atmosphere. "Well, well, well," Eve said, eyeing Noah, "this isn't my usual café. I hope the coffee here doesn't taste like dishwater." Noah chuckled, rising to greet her. "Eve, you're a lifesaver."

As Eve approached, her gaze swept the room, finally landing on Mike's slumped figure. Her expression transformed from playful to puzzled. "Mike? What's he doing here at this ungodly hour? He's just a child! Shouldn't he be in school?" Noah gestured for Eve to sit. "Long story, Eve. Mike's been having some...interesting dreams." Eve's eyebrows shot up. "Interesting? That's code for 'terrifying,' right?" Noah filled Eve in on Mike's dream, the glass, and the toy car and how everything felt real. Eve's expression turned serious.

"Let me take a look," Eve said, pulling out her forensic kit. As Eve examined the glass and toy car, Mike remained motionless, his back to Eve. "Mike, kiddo, what's wrong?" Eve asked, concern creeping into her voice. Noah intervened. "He's just shaken up."

Eve's eyes scanned the glass and toy car, her brow furrowed in concentration. Finally, she looked up, a mixture of surprise and curiosity on her face. "No fingerprints," Eve announced, her voice tinged with puzzlement. "Not a single one."

Mike's gaze lifted, hope and confusion warring on his face. "What does it mean?" Eve's expression softened as she approached Mike. "It means it was just a nightmare, kiddo. A vivid dream. Your mind's been playing tricks" Mike's shoulders slumped, relief and disappointment mingling. Eve wrapped a reassuring arm around Mike. "Come on, I'll have my driver take you home. You need rest." As Mike stood, Eve handed him a gentle smile. "You're safe now, Mike. Just forget this ever happened."

Noah watched as Eve ushered Mike out of the café, his mind whirling with questions. Once they were gone, Noah pulled out his laptop and motioned for Eve to sit beside him. "Time to compare notes," Noah said, his eyes locked on Eve's. Eve settled in, her own laptop open. "I've been digging into Andrea's disappearance. Found some interesting connections."

Noah's eyebrows rose. "What kind of connections?" Eve's gaze flicked to the screen. "Similar cases in nearby towns. All girls, same age range. No leads, no suspects." Noah's expression darkened. "Sounds like a pattern." Eve nodded. "And then there's Mike's dream. No fingerprints, no evidence. Just a haunting sense of familiarity with reality."

CHAPTER FOURTEEN

THE SIXTH SENSE

"Hey guys! Are you having a coffee date without me?" "B-Brennan, you-?" "Oh yeah I just happened to pass by" he chuckled. "So, this was a pure coincidence, isn't it?" Eve laughed breaking the uncomfortable silence among them.

"Not really... I just wanted to visit the headquarters to collect some research papers, but when I called the manager to book a driver, she told me that the driver was already booked by you. I wondered where you had to go this late so, I came here myself" He chuckled as he sat down on the next chair at the table. "So... what were you guys doing here?" "Oh! We were just exchanging our articles on some related researches" "On Andrea's case, huh?" "Yeah! We just happened to share similar ideas, see this" Eve slid her laptop over to him.

After a long conversation everybody departed for their respective homes. "You can go with the driver I'll drop Noah" Brennan smiled as he started his car and waved a goodbye to her.

'He is cute sometimes' Eve blushes speaking to herself. "Let's go now".

'Oh my! Look at this innocent in this dark night, thought he could escape my eyes... He lived for enough, I hope his death

causes pain and fear' smiled the unknown as it vanished into the thin air imagining the worst.

Later that morning, traffic broke out on highway near savannah river, it wasn't a normal traffic but caused something more tragic and unexpected than ever. "When are you pulling out the car" Edwin's consciousness kicked in. "We are trying sir, maybe in a short time we'll get to know who was inside" "You better do your work quickly"

"Oh, sorry if we were late" Brennan took a deep breath as he handed over the conversation to Eve. "There was traffic on our way here, I mean you should just appreciate our compassion for our work that we came running around 500m!" Eve gasped. "Whatever!" As time passed by everyone impatiently staired the river, with no sign of moment. "We found the car!" The pully truck's driver informed the inspectors. "Hurry up and get it out!" Edwin yelled as he was getting more impatient second by second"

After some 5 minutes of struggle finally the car was safely pulled out of the river, by the look of the car one could easily tell that it had crashed into the water brutally. "Oh god!" Everyone gasped seeing the pitiful view.

As the pully put the car down investigation team surrounded it with eyes on the car searching for damages and making intuitions. "So, there was only one guy in the car, who was driving, looking at his face won't help us we can't recognize his blue and swollen face" Brennan mumbled. "Eve, check his car's interior and his clothes, it's better if he has his ID card. We can recognize his Identity." Eve rushed towards the car searching every pocket and corner as at last she found an identity card in his blazer's pocket.

Her jaw dropped as she couldn't believe what she was seeing. 'I-Its Mr. Lewin" she gasped in shock. "Wait! Isn't he the father of the high school boy we sent to juvenile for Andrea's case?" Edwin doubted his assumption trying to confirm it again. "y-yes" Eve stuttered. "I don't think we can do any further assumptions here in this surrounding, I wish to see the team in headquarters at 12" Edwin ordered them as he continued talking with another inspector on the crime scene and completing some formalities and paper work.

"What do you think it was a murder or just an accident?" Eve asked in curiosity. "I don't want to state anything before we investigate the accident" Brennan sighed. "Let's go now, I think sir can handle this" Noah interrupted them as he indicated towards his car. They all were tired due to less sleeping hours yesterday, and thus, decided to rest for sometimes before the investigation goes on.

Everyone was on time, of course they never liked being scolded by Edwin for their timelessness. "What do you all think about this? Is there anyone who can explain this?" Edwin asked sarcastically as he knew nobody had the answer to his question. "I think I know something"

Noah stood up from his place as his last night conversations kicked in. "Can't you connect the dots too?" he asked Eve and Brennan. "You were with me when Mike told me his dream" He pointed towards Eve. "Yeah, I was... but why do you think about that now?" "Because in his dreams Andrea drowned a car into the glass of water!" "So, what!?" "Can't you connect the chain of incidents!? By that Andrea wanted to warn us about her next move! The car in his dream, in reality depicted his father's car and the glass of water, the river" Noah breath in sharply after completing the sentence in flow.

"Do you want us to believe in some child's so called precognitive dream?" Edwin sighed in frustration. "Weren't you with me last night!? Didn't you saw the fear in Mike's eyes as if he was telling the raw truth?" "Yeah, I know that" Eve mumbled. "If it is true... I guess we'll need some help" Edwin's eyes were locked onto Noah. "And from whom-?" "I think of that old man, Ezra" "yeah, I think he can help us telling some more details about such precognitive dreams" Brennan's mind kicked in. "So, are we going to Mist woods again?" Eve sighed.

"I don't think we all have spare time to visit together again. I'll be staying here." Edwin informs everyone with a dull gaze, not as usual. "But-" "I have some legal documentation work so I can't leave the city for some days, but you guys can go there if you want, that too for not more than a week!" He smiled genuinely as he left the room with some uncleared doubts and confusions.

"So, it'll be three of us going this time?" "yeah" "no problem I'll book the bus" Noah checked his phone for booking the bus. "He gave us a week, so we have to complete our investigation in just a week" Eve sighed as she held her head with her hands in place trying to process the mess going on in their investigation.

"Did you forget what happened when we last visited there?" Brennan was horrified by the mere existence of the village's name in their conversation. "I still remember that... but we can't just let go! It's our responsibility to find out about Andrea's current state. We don't even know what she is or where she is! Her mother is dead and father is in depression! Now, even Mike's dad is gone... poor child, we don't even know what he must be going through." Eve cried out her feelings. "We can't really do anything about a girl who is not even a human!" Brennan tries to prove his point.

"I've booked the bus for tomorrow evening" Noah break in their argument trying to normalize the situation.

CHAPTER FIFTEEN

ONCE MORE

They were all lost in their minds, when, out of nowhere, a white-tailed deer sprang onto their path, the driver lost control and the bus crashed into the forest. Everyone was shocked by the sudden crash and suddenly looked at each other hoping that everyone is safe. "I-Is everyone okay!?" Brennan cleared his throat looking at the pale faces of everyone. "Yeah" "But what was this!?" "A white-tailed deer sprang on our path, I-I just lost controls of the bus" The driver sighed in guilt. "I am glad everyone was safe" Noah cried in relief.

"How long is the journey ahead?" "I think 1-2 hours still to go..." Noah was frustrated by the fact that it was getting dark and still they had not reached his village. "Would you like to eat this?" Eve changed the topic slightly and handed over the box of cookies to Brennan and Noah. "Oh, thanks" they both took a bite and leaned back in their seats. "Are you sure Ezra would be still there in the village?" "I think so, I can't say anything about that" Noah stated, his voice just above a whisper.

"So, Andrea's brother was sent to hostel, right?" Eve wanted to clear her doubts. "Yeah, but why do you ask?" Brennan replied in cold voice. "Just wanted to make sure he is safe" "So, she has a brother too?" Noah asked as he had never met her brother and joined the case after some while. "Yup, she has"

Hours passed and they finally reached the mist woods, "Shall we go to my house, I think we all need some rest, we can find Ezra tomorrow" Noah suggested as they all walked in his house. "Eve you can use the room on 1ˢᵗ floor, we will take rooms on the ground floor" "Okay, thanks!" Eve dragged her bags to the first floor and settled herself on the bed, unpacking some stuff"

"Are you new here?" a sharp sound hit Eve's consciousness as she turned around to the window and reached out herself. She saw a beautiful lady in the next house peeking in through her window. "N-no, it's just my friend's house" Eve smiled at the lady on the next window trying to be calm. "Oh, I see. Noah didn't tell me he had friends, after all his family has been through, I never saw him in the village. Ezra sent him in the city, I think he missed his village" She smiled mysteriously. "The last time we visited here, you weren't home, right?" "No, I was here only watching you every day" she chuckled. Her words sent shivers in Eve's body. "I want you to keep a little secret to yourself" The lady asked Eve. "What is it?" "Promise me you won't tell anyone that you talked with me, or we ever met like this" Eve was shocked at her plead yet she agreed not wanting to ask questions on her weird request. "I wouldn't" Eve smiled at her making her assure.

Eve heard some footsteps approaching her room, she turned to look if Noah was here, she saw no one. But as she looked outside the window again, the lady was gone, with her windows closed too. "weird" she mumbled and closed her window too and went to sleep.

The next morning the trio went into the woods to look for Ezra, they reached his cottage and knocked the door. "Come in" they slowly opened the creaky door and stepped in. "as usual Ezra was having a cup of coffee sitting in his lawn chair, as sunlight added a glow on his face "Hello sir!" Ezra nodded as he indicated them to sit and looked at Eve with a mysterious glance.

"How did you know we were at the door?" Brennan asked as he sat down. "The spirits of forest tell me everything they see" he chuckled as he took a sip from his coffee. Everyone was shocked at his delusional reply but no one dared to question him about that. "Actually, we wanted to ask about-" "about that child's dream?" Ezra looked at them his eyes reflecting the truth he had already known. "How d-do you know about that?" "I already told you how" Ezra smiled at them. "But what is the relation of forest's spirits with the boy's dream?" Noah asked hoping to get an answer by asking the same delusional questions to Ezra. "The water in his dream, in the glass, was an element of the forest itself" Ezra smiled at them. "But the car drowned in Savannah River" Brennan sighed. "That's what you think..." Ezra sighed and stood up from his chair. "So, can you tell us about his precognitive dream?" Eve stated their main question. "That was a warning" "Warning from?" "From either the guardian of spirits or from Andrea" Ezra looked at them his eyes filled with truthfulness and believe.

"As we expected" Brennan mumbled. "The carnival of forest is near, I don't suggest you leaving the forest till the celebration is over" Ezra told them, his voice just above a whisper. "When is that carnival?" "Day after the following day" Ezra brought some cherries from his kitchen and started walking out of the house.

No one dared to question him as they watched him through the window. He placed the basket there and stepped in. "Shall we talk later?" Ezra asked as he walked them outside his house and waved them a farewell. "Weird than before" Eve mumbled as they all started walking outside the forest, asking Noah about the annually celebrated carnival.

As they reached home, everyone got busy with their usual morning routine and spent the rest of the day in their office work and reports. The sun was already below the horizon, Eve was still working on her laptop, when a sudden voice caught her attention. "Hey! What are you doing" this time again, the voice came from the next house. Eve slowly climbed up to the window and looked outside, she saw that lady again. "Oh hey!" she replied. "You seem to be tired, I bet you are working from the whole day" "yeah, I was just busy in some office work" Eve smiled at her. "Wanna go on a walk with me?" The lady offered Eve. "No problem!" Eve chuckled at the lady's sudden request. "Then meet me at the fountain in 10 minutes" The lady smiled at Eve.

After some 10 minutes Eve left the house without telling anyone about where she was going, she covered herself in a shawl wanting to resist the cold temperature in the village. She saw the lady at the fountain already waiting for her. "Did you tell anyone about this?" The lady asked as Eve approached her. "No" Eve chuckled as she offered her hand to the lady. "Well, that's good" The lady smiled back as they both began walking around the town.

"So, what's your name?" "It's Daizy" The lady smiles. "Why is the village so empty?" Eve asked as she looked around and saw no one. "It is not like cities where people roam around late night, and on top of all, Carnival is near"

Daizy continued walking. "What do you mean by carnival is near?" "I mean the people don't dare to walk late nights when carnival is coming, they consider it as a bad luck in life." Daizy slowed down her walking pace. "A bad luck?" Eve's eyes widened in surprise.

"It is believed in the nights of carnival week forest spirits go under enhancement and thus, the village is left unprotected as the spirits' energy is weakened, during this time of the year, people are likely to get disappeared during night time" Daizy chuckled. Daizy's words sent shivers down her spine as she continued walking. "What if we get caught?" Eve gulped in fear. "Not we dear, it will be you..." Daizy chuckled sinisterly.

Eve stopped walking beside her and stood in her place still shocked with what Daizy just said. "w-what do you mean!?" Eve gasped. "Just joking, don't be scared" Daizy laughed. Eve took a deep breathe, "you almost got me off guard" Eve chuckled trying to normalize the situation.

Suddenly a familiar voice catches Eve's attention, she turned around and saw Noah, half asleep calling out to her standing in front of the main door. "I think I have to go" Eve looked back at Daizy. Her jaw dropped at the scene. Daizy wasn't there but instead there was a low cold breeze. "weird" Eve mumbled as she looked around for a while and then approached Noah.

"What were you doing outside?" Noah asked rubbing his eyes, trying to see properly. "Just having a walk" "And why were you talking to yourself?" Noah raised an eyebrow. "No! I was on a walk with your neighbor but when I saw you and then I saw her, she was gone... Isn't it weird?" Eve sighed and went inside to her room. "My neighbor? Do I even have one!?" Noah mumbled to himself and went to sleep as he was half asleep. Eve squirm on her bed still thinking about the strange lady. "She always disappears like this" Eve sighed in frustration as she closed her eyes, trying to sleep. It was of no use. she was not sleepy yet she was lying there over thinking about what she talked or listened.

'Maybe I should stop thinking delusionally and try to sleep' she talked to herself turning sides. It was almost 2 AM and she was still changing sides, half asleep. Tired of wanting to sleep. It was for sure the longest night for Eve.

CHAPTER SIXTEEN

HALLUCINATION

The sun rises and so does George, he steps outside the house and takes a deep breath and does a morning stretch. "Wake up!" he shakes Noah a bit, trying to wake him up. Noah sat down at his place still trying to process his surroundings. "I am making some coffee so get up and you better come out within 10 minutes" Brennan sighed as he left the room and gave a miss call to Eve to wake her up too. Eve got startled by the sudden call and wakes up, "It would have been nice of him, if he, himself would have come to wake me up" Eve mumbled to herself.

She got up from her bed, scratching her head while trying to remember last night's incident. She walked downstairs as she found Brennan making some coffee. "Thankyou" She whispered as Brennan put a cup of coffee in front of her on the table.

The whole day passed on like the previous day, it was evening when Eve's consciousness kicked in and she got up from her place stretching her body muscles as she had been sitting there for hours working on her laptop.

"I'm going for a walk" She announced to Brennan and Noah, as she stepped out. She could saw people talking and walking on the streets as they were decorating the village for tomorrow's carnival. As she was walking, she sat down near the same fountain where she met Daizy the previous night. "She doesn't show up during evening..." Eve mumbled to herself talking about the lady.

Suddenly she felt someone's presence beside her, it was Ezra. "Oh, hey! How come you decided to visit the village today" She was shocked as she stood up from her place and looked at him. "I wanted to talk about someone" "About whom?" Eve looked curious. "About the lady you were on a walk with yesterday" Ezra sighed. "Ho do y-you know?" Eve was shocked as she stuttered a bit. "Because she wasn't real" Ezra looked at her with a calm reaction. "Wasn't real!? What do you mean by that?" Eve's eyes widened at his reaction.

"She was a negative element, who succeeded in disguising itself in human form, you should be thankful you were saved last night" Ezra continued clearing her doubts. "You mean that's the reason she denied me from telling anyone about our meetings" "Possibly yeah..." Ezra sighed in relief. She was horrified as she replayed her memories with that lady last night, she slowly realized the reason of her weirdness, why she disappeared suddenly and why she talked in a weird tone with her.

"So, it was my hallucination?" "It can be" "You mean no one could see her except me?" she was shocked. "I don't think so anyone else saw her except you" Ezra had the same calm reaction on his face. "Thanks for telling me this sir, I have some doubts to clear so I'll be get going then!" She rushed away from the fountain and reached the house panting and breathing heavily.

She saw Noah sitting in the lawn with his laptop, she immediately ran up to him. "Hey! Do you remember what happened last night!?" She began with her point. "When you were walking down the streets?" he scratched his head trying to know what she wanted to ask. "Yup, so... did you see anyone walking with me?" "Nope, that's why I wondered what were you doing alone at that hour" "Do you know anything about your neighbor named Daizy?" She was getting curious and wanted to clear her doubts.

"Aunt Daizy? Huh?" he asked her back "How do you know about her?" he continued his question. "You mean you know her!? Is she for real?" she was shocked with his reply. "Dude, she passed away when I was 10" He chuckled. "But why do you ask? I mean from where did you get her name?" "n-nothing..." she was all confused and terrified that she couldn't explain his question.

"She had long black hairs, and a middle nose piercing with thin braids throughout her hair?" She asked to get a clear idea of her. "Yeah, but when she got aged, she changed her style, but how did you know!? You saw her photo, Isn't it?" "No! I saw her with my damn eyes!" She panted as she didn't want to admit anything like that. "What did you just say?" Noah was shocked as she confessed something weird than what he was expecting.

"You heard me!" she was breathing sharply, feeling out of breath, she held her head with her hands trying to breath calmly. "b-but how!?" Noah was getting tensed. "I-I don't know! Why did she come? What did she want from me? I just d-don't know anything" she was breathing heavily feeling dizzy. "Just calm down! Okay? We'll talk about this later if you're not feeling okay" Noah got up from his seat as he went into the kitchen to get some water for her.

She was not in her right mind, she felt heaviness in her chest as she fainted slowly sitting down next to the wall, slipping down the corner, her vision blurred with fear and confusion. The last thing she saw was Noah running towards her and shaking her trying to keep her awake.

It was now almost 2 hours since Eve last woke up, she slowly opened her eyes and found herself in bed at ground floor's room. "How do you feel?" she saw an unknown figure in front of her, it was a nurse. "I-I am okay" she slowly sat up on the bed scratching her head which was still a bit heavy. As she turned her gaze around the room, she saw Brennan sitting there looking a bit tensed.

"You had a panic attack" the nurse told her grabbing her attention. Brennan nodded after the nurse trying to keep his reaction normal. "Noah told me you fainted near kitchen, so he went to call a nurse from the local village hospital, leaving me with you to take your care" Brennan sighed as he looked up at Eve. "So, he told you the reason?" "Yeah, he did. But he too was not sure about anything and told me that when you'll wake up you will tell the rest of the details" confusion etched on his face as he tilted his face.

"c-can I have some water?" "Oh, sure" he handed over a glass of water to her. "So, would you like to tell the rest of the part?" Brennan came to the point. "Noah told me Daizy was his aunt who lived in the next house, she was a bit aged, but when I saw her, she was a young lady with beautiful features. I saw her for the first time when she called me out at the window just the day when we came here, she told me not to tell anyone about her" Eve was tensed and horrified. "It's okay, breathe evenly if you don't want a panic attack again" Brennan tried to mock her, normalizing the heaviness in the surroundings.

"I met Ezra today, he knew I was with that woman last night, ho too told me she wasn't real" she sighed. "But how did he know? Was he with you?" "N-no, he just told me he can feel that negative energy" "That old man surely isn't something easy to understand!" Brennan smirked.

"Oh, you're awake" Noah came into the room. Eve looked at him "Sorry for the trouble I caused" "It's okay, now you better start taking care of your health" Noah smiled politely. "Oh yeah!" she laughed at herself. "I'll tell you the remaining details" Brennan told Noah as he took him out of the room leaving Eve with the nurse.

"Hey miss? What about my payment?" The nurse stated rudely. "Oh sorry, I forgot to ask about that" She took out her phone and made an online payment. The nurse left after getting her payment. "If they tried to help me then why didn't they pay for the medication fee!? Stingy people!" she mumbled to herself in frustration.

"Hey! Wake up" Brennan shake her a bit. "Oh, when did I sleep" she woke up in blurry vision. "I don't know that, but you can't sleep on my bed, go to your room" Brennan ordered her like a stubborn kid. "Oops, sorry I'll be get going then" she chuckled to herself. She picked up her stuff and went upstairs.

After some while a knock approached her room's door. "Come in" "you forgot the dinner, just eat this. You'll feel better" Brennan looked down as he placed the plate on the table and left the room without saying anything. 'He is weird sometimes too' Eve smiled to herself as she got up to take her food.

CHAPTER SEVENTEEN

FIRST CELEBRATION

It was the next day, not just a usual day, but the carnival's first day. The carnival festival was a 3-day long celebration and today was the first celebration. "What should I wear?" Eve rushed downstairs to get some opinions. "Whatever you want to" Brennan sighed not even looking at her. "Just help me choose from these two" she showed him the both dresses in excitement. "We are going there just as a formality, you know it, right?" he finally looked up at her. "Whatever!" she pouted at him and went upstairs to her room beating the ground with heavy footsteps. Brennan laughed at her immature behavior as he continued his article.

"So, we'll be leaving at 4 PM. The main celebrations begin at that time. Please remember, you mustn't take any food item from anyone and if you do then don't bring it back home. The most important thing is that you won't go to the forest at the time of rituals and celebration, am I clear?" Noah puts his points altogether. "Is Ezra coming?" Brennan asked. "I don't think so, he never visited these celebrations since my brother was taken" Noah looked down at his foot, he was tapping it impatiently due to nervousness. "Don't get anxious, I don't want any other guy to faint here" Brennan laughed as he indirectly mocked Eve's weakness. "Hey! What are you trying to prove!" Eve was furious as she looked away due to embarrassment. "I am just joking guys" Brennan forcefully stopped himself bursting in laugh.

After some time, the village was lightened up due to thousands of lanterns glowing inside, it was now the time as the celebration begun with a short collective prayer. "What should we do? We don't even know the prayer!" Eve whispered to Brennan. "Just close your eyes and bow your head down" he told her as they did the same.

Just before the priest could throw the holocaust a sudden burst of light caught everyone's attention, everything went silent. "what's there!" A man shouted from the crowd as everybody turned their gaze towards the forest. "Oh, no!" Noah shouted as he ran towards the light. "Where do you think you are going!?" Brennan shouted as he sprinted towards him wanting him to stop.

The crowd got terrified and a stampede took place, everyone ran towards their home, children were crying, while parents were terrified looking for their lost children. Fire broke out as lanterns broke and the dry grasses caught fire, winds blew harder, extinguishing the holy fire at the ritual place, Eve struggled herself out of the stampede, "What's with them now!" She got worried and ran after them. Noah stopped before Ezra's cottage, "I knew this" He rushed inside, followed by Brennan and Eve. "Where are you going!?" Brennan shouted from behind. Noah searched every corner of his house. He was not there. "Where's he now!" he got tensed and came out.

"Oh, no!" he looked at the wild fire breaking into some houses and forest. "What are you up to!?" Eve was tensed as she was panting. "See that deer!" Noah pointed out a white-tailed deer peeking at them from the forest. "He is familiar one" Noah ran after the deer as the deer sprang into the forest, almost disappearing. "Wait for us!" they both ran behind Noah.

They were panting and breathing heavily as they ran behind the deer. The deer got vanished and all they could see there was Ezra coughing, sitting next to a tree. "The c-cat" he whispered trying to breathe in. "What's with the cat now?" Eve squatted near him patting his back. "It got angry, it ran a-away" he coughed more.

"The village's on fire sir!" Brennan was out of breath as he breath sharply. "Worry about the people! It would take them!" Ezra yelled at them. "It would take whom?" Noah was horrified by the look of village and the forest. "It would take e-eleven people from the village, save them" he coughed more. "But how can w-we?" Eve was stressed out. "Just make sure the holy fire is alive-" "It's not" Eve looked down interrupting him. "We are done, I-I'm sorry, we couldn't save them" Ezra looked at the moon as tears rolled down his cheeks. "Sir! Are you sure this was the only way?" Brennan was refusing himself to lose hope.

"There is... but we can't reach it" "reach what?" "Reach the temple!" he coughed a bit. "The t-temple? But no one has seen the temple in decades" Noah sighed in stress. "I know, that's why we can't save the people now" he looked up trying to hold back his tears of guilt.

The crowd's noise was still piercing through their ears, their horrified scream pricked their hearts with guilt and helplessness. "Come on sir" Brennan supported Ezra to stand up and walk with him, Noah and Eve followed them as they reached Ezra's house in some minutes. "We will come back sir, take care" Brennan sighed in frustration as he told Eve to stay here and look after him.

Noah and George left for the village, helping the people to extinguish fire, and to rescue people out of it. Helping the kids to reach out to their parents and helping women to keep themselves safe. They guided the crowd to the north of village, where the fire had not reached yet.

"Is everyone safe now!?" Brennan raised his voice trying to reach to every person's alertness. The crowd cross talked their decisions and settled there for a while. "Why did this happen?" Brennan turned his gaze onto Noah trying to have some clue. "I-I don't know" "Then why did you ran to the forest like you knew everything from the beginning?" "I ran in there because the light blew up from the direction of Ezra's house, I was sure it must be related to him, that's why..." Noah sighed trying to catch some breath but the air was filled with smoke, which was choking him. "The village's southern part has turned into ash... do you have any plans now?" Brennan looked up at Noah trying to get some positive response. "N-no" He went numb, trying to process out everything.

They both rushed out of the area, with red irritating eyes and coughs which slowly cut their oxygen. "Eve must be still in forest" Brennan looked up to Noah who was still gasping for air. He slightly nodded as they both dragged themselves out of smoke, into the northern part.

Eve was still with Ezra, in his house, which was located in the southern-most part of the village, mostly in the deep forest grounds. Where the low growls of wild animals fill the air with their not-so pleasing music. The villagers haven't experienced such kind of environment as never did they try to wander around the forests at night.

Eve rested in the living room her mind raced with fear and confusion for the incidents that she experienced till now, she was also deeply traumatized with the existence of Daizy, a woman who appeared out of nowhere and then just disappeared and never be seen again.

Her thoughts and questions were far more than anyone could listen to or answer to. She did want to clear some doubts but decided not to cause pain to Ezra as he was already injured... it did seem mystery for them to unfold after the chain of incidents which they've been through since they came here. Nothing was normal, everything got more complex after they came here for the second time.

She lay down on the couch as she stared at the ceiling, her breathing was uneven, her eyes not blinking as she stared at the roof for long. She was there but her mind raced with thoughts of another place, thoughts of other people which she'd encountered in her life since the case was being assigned to her team. The case wasn't as normal as the ones her team always solved within few weeks.

It's been 3 months now, they haven't had any information, it was like the mystery was getting dry by the time they struggled to find proofs and evidences, seems like their investigation and research was going in vain as the case's progress almost slowed down and stopped.

They came here when they were lost in their own lives and lived like some ordinary people unaware of such things which happened in the same world as they were living in. Andrea's case was filled with so much confusions and relations that it happened to be seen as a story on its own.

CHAPTER EIGHTEEN

THE
DESTRUCTION

She never realized when her thoughts led to sleep and she slept there, on the couch. As sunlight peaked in through the window creaks, some hit her face with warmth and calmness unlike the atmosphere that surrounded the villagers, the atmosphere which was filled with confusions and fear among them.

Her eyes, now wide open as she stood up and realized how her hallucinations turned into deep sleep. She scratched her head and went to see Ezra's condition and check on his health status. She approached his room and knocked a few times, no response- she then opened the door quietly peaking in to see Ezra.

He wasn't there, sleeping in his room as he was expected to be seen. She looked around the whole room to make sure he was not inside. She then searched the living room and the rooms upstairs as when finally, she came down and opened the window, here he was! Sitting in a lawn chair sipping a cup of coffee. "You almost scared me!" She chuckled as she walked towards him. "Did I?" he laughed back as if trying to start a normal conversation instead of discussing the events from last night. "How're the villagers now?" He asked making her forget about the questions she was about to ask.

"I-I don't know if you really ask me about that, I haven't had contact with Noah or George after they left us both here and went towards village." Eve sighs as her consciousness shifted towards the thought of villagers and their most probably destroyed village and home. A tensed environment started to build around them as they both sit there silently watching the sun come up.

"You can have something made for you in the kitchen, I bet you didn't have any dinner" Ezra finally spoke to her trying to have a light environment as he shifted in his chair and glanced towards her. "Oh yeah!" she got up from the stairs and went inside to find something ready to eat, she didn't want to make a mess in someone else's kitchen.

After having some regular bread, she picked up her things from the couch "I have to leave now... I want to check on my friends, you can call me if you need anything" She smiled and walked away without waiting for any response. She closed the door behind her and headed towards north, to the village. Her mind already recalling the questions she had for them.

She didn't bother to ask Ezra about last night as she knew it would be better to leave him alone in there, instead of questioning him like some prisoner. She walked through the forest and reached the southern entrance of village, the view was terrifying, houses were destroyed and almost burned down, trees were on the streets spreading their broken branches and half burnt leaves all through the pathways, as she walked, crushing the leaves coming in her way and sliding the stems away from her foot.

No on was there, 'Oh god what happened here!?' she thought to herself gasping in air while trying to calculate the effects of aftermath. She walked continuously until she reached the northern part and saw few people crying and talking nearby. 'So, everyone's in the north, thank god they're safe' she thought to herself as her eyes began searching for the two she was looking for.

Her roaming eyes fell under a tree where they both were sitting and talking, without wasting any second she rushed towards them, "Hey!?" she came grabbing their attention as she waved her one hand in air. They both looked her coming but didn't bother to reply anything.

"How are you two?" she asked catching some breath. "Fine..." Noah replied with a sigh. "We aren't the one you should be tensed about, just look at the villagers and their houses in south burnt down" Brennan frowned. "I saw that" she replied with pity as she sat beside them crossing her legs and leaning on her arms behind her. "So, what about the other 2 days of carnival?" she asked.

"I talked about it from some locals, they'll be cancelling the prayers this year and instead of that, they'll maybe sacrifice one animal or two, just to make sure their lord is happy and satisfied" Noah sighed in pity for the animal that would be possibly sacrificed for some little play of forgiveness and enchantment.

"So, tell us what he said" "I didn't ask him anything related to last night's incident" she replied her eyes still fixed on kids playing. "I thought it wouldn't be right to ask him about anything what happened, he looked disturbed, he tried to hide his emotions playing cool, I get him" She continued.

"Alright" Brennan sighed as they all were lost in their own thoughts and imaginations. After spending sometime

Eve stood up and turned around, "I think we all should get some rest... I know last night wasn't expected to be like that but we just can't sit here weeping about the sorrows of villagers all day long!" her sudden statement gave her the attention she wanted to make herself clear.

"We can't let such incidents traumatize us! It's been our work to handle tough situations with no mercy at all! I know we are humans too, but instead of watching them like this, we should call cops to help them!" she stated in a single breath as some unfamiliar voice break in their conversation. "Miss, you can't call any stranger or outsider during carnival season and especially not any cop" As they looked behind to catch a sight of the warning giver, they saw an old lady, she was wearing a red muffler around her neck and a long heavy coat hung over her shoulders, by her looks one could easily say she looked in her 80s, her tone was more like some warning, she appeared out of nowhere, which made her look even more mysterious.

Eve maintained her figure and nodded not wanting to argue with some old lady, randomly. She again observed the two figures sitting against her "Do you plan on sitting there for the day?" she taunted, making a frustrated face.

"Yeah sure" Brennan stood up and followed her as they retire to Noah's house. Without glancing back at them Eve directly proceeded upstairs making less to almost no sounds. Her movements clearly stated she was too tired to talk to them, everyone retired to bed.

Eve flopped in her bed as she stared out of window, her eyes fixed there, for a little longer. As she was trying to recall the conversations she shared with Daizy, never did she imagine Daizy wasn't a real person. This thought made her even more insecure of her surroundings, she started doubting the world and people around her.

After squirming for a while she finally sat up, knowing that she won't be able to sleep today, she went downstairs. Her movements were slow as she walked on toes trying not to make any noise. She approached the living room where she saw Brennan already sitting there with his eyes fixed on the laptop screen before him.

"Insomnia?"

"Yeah..." he replied with a sigh, he continued "Why are you awake?" "I was also having trouble sleeping tonight" she chuckled, scratching the back of her head as she sat beside him catching a glimpse of the laptop screen. He was typing some reports, his fingers gliding over the keyboard smoothly yet lively. "Article?" "Nope, I'm just updating the milestone and reports of Andrea Holmes" he sighed, his eyes still on screen.

Eve sat there watching his work and reports and recalling the milestones they made till now in the case. The lights were off and the only light came through the laptop fell on their faces, enabling them to maintain focus on it. As he finished writing he stretched his arms in air, leaning back into the chair. "I think you should just sleep" he looked up at the time and then Eve. "I'm not sleepy" she let herself fall back in chair.

He looked at her for a while and then opened another while in his tab and started studying some article. She was still sitting there watching the screen and processing out the article he was reading. "What's this?" she whispered. "It's some crime article and records" his eyes were still focused on screen.

"Best of luck, sleeping!" she spoke in a mocking tone as she stood up and climbed the stairs up to her room leaving him in the living room like he was before. She jumped on her bed trying to sleep, so that she doesn't have to spend a night accompanying a boring person and his boring task.

CHAPTER NINETEEN

TRAUMATIZED

'Mike's not been eating properly since Mr. Lewin passed away, he is always scared and quiet, he doesn't even speak to anyone else. He just sits in his room and only comes out for food, they shifted him out of juvenile as per the orders so we sent a nurse to look after him, to maintain his reports and health records, but the nurse's been giving some shocking reports since she moved in with him. We don't know much but she says he is always locked up in his room, he doesn't talk to anyone or attends his appointments with psychologists.'

"See this!" Eve rushed downstairs into the living room shouting through the staircase as she reached the table and saw Brennan sleeping with his head on table. Without wasting any time, she shook him as he wakes up, startled.

"See these reports, Director Rachel sent these to me this morning!" She immediately shoved her phone to his side, which displayed the message on screen. He started reading the message, rubbing his eyes, trying to see properly after a messy sleep cycle.

'Nurse's been telling us that he always locks up himself in his room before evening and then comes out the next morning for breakfast, most of the times he skips dinner. He never listens to nurse and is always tired when he comes out for

meals, his face is always dull and dark circles made his eyes look even more scary... I personally took the boy for his appointment, the doctor believes the reason is depression or maybe he is in some trauma, I think that is a possible reason for a boy to be traumatized after losing his father in some sudden manner. I just felt to give the information as the case is been handled by your team and I won't tolerate any weak points!'

They both looked at the message and then each other, they were numb from the news as somehow, they did have an idea of his health status, of course it's too traumatizing to lose your father at a young age, and when his mother is not with him too. "Poor boy" Brennan exhaled. "I'll take his doctor's contact number from Miss Rachel to have his reports in hand, I'll then try to plan a healthy schedule for him to get better." Eve sighed as she messaged Miss Rachel just after that and went away typing in her phone, standing next to a window.

Brennan stood up and stretched his arms in air as he went to wake up Noah, "Hey bud! Wake up" he shook him till he was wide awake. "Something wrong?" Noah yawned as he gets up from the bed. "Yeah, just some mental health problems, Mike Lewin you remember?" "Yup! So, he isn't well..." Noah narrowed his eyes for a second making eye contact with Brennan, waiting for a reply.

"Eve will handle her job, now get up and make me some breakfast" Brennan walked out of his room as a smirked played on his lips. "Make a what? You woke me up just because you were hungry?" Noah yelled at him as he followed him to the living room. "Well, aren't we as a guest here?" Brennan gave him a cocky smile as he indicated him to cook some eggs.

Noah sighed and started making some boiled eggs with salad. Brennan was on his phone, checking some updates as he sat down on chair next to him like he's been checking if he cooks properly or not. After awhile Eve joined them at table, still texting someone.

"Looks delicious" she finally turned away her gaze from phone and looked at the table where the breakfast lied. "I got his number, I've asked for the reports... let's see when will I get them" She smiled at the food, and started eating it like she was hungry for days! "Slow down, you'll choke" Noah chuckled at her eating pace. "Yeah, he's right, we can't afford you passing out again" Brennan started laughing humorlessly accompanied by bravo taps on his shoulder by Noah. Eve chuckled too, not wanting to make the joke serious by minding it.

"By the way... which reports were you talking about right now?" Noah looked up at her. "Oh! Right, I'll forward you the message Miss Rachel sent me." He nodded as they continued with their breakfast for some while.

"Let's stop pretending what we already know" Brennan sighed as he played with his food in plate. The sudden and strange comment left both of them startled. "We all know Andrea's alive" he continued "She's been murdering people and with the fact she can regenerate! I don't accept her as a human anymore!" his tone was shaky as he dropped his fork on plate.

"The amount of murder cases in our city has risen up tremendously. At first, I thought it was some mafia group or murderers, but you know what I've been studying since days!? The cases themselves! Each murder was happened cruelly, where the cops couldn't even find bodies sometimes! The only thing on spot was blood that stained tiles badly, and the amount of blood seen every time is so much that if one person bleeds that much there isn't any chance of him being alive!" he growled.

Eve's jaw dropped at his sudden research results as she was numb to speak anything, "You think Andrea killed so many people on her own?" Noah squirmed in his seat trying to get comfortable. "Yes! indeed. She isn't some humanly strength anymore, she's even way too clever that she never leaves trails behind her murders so that anyone could track her or even understand anything properly."

"We are swimming in two boats, who knows if we might slip off from one or other?" Eve finally spoke. "First we only had Andrea's case to solve, and now, after coming in this village, there is a whole different yet connective story going on!" she lets out her frustration which pierced her heart till the very day. "Do we even have any plan what to do next instead of scrolling through some articles and research papers?" the environment was getting heavy with her continuous questions but no answers in return.

By some time she realized, the numbness on their faces, she knew even they don't know the answer to her doubts which were too confusing to get away from. "You're right, we don't have plans this time..." finally Brennan replied with heavy heart and a low voice, seeming like the mutter was more to himself than any other in this room.

"I know this place helped us to have a better perspective on this case, which on our own, we could never develop, I know our lives and the case has gotten more complex than before" Noah sighed trying to keep both sides of the coin in check.

"Do you think sir Simpson can handle all those cases alone?" Eve looked up at both of them.

"I don't think so, since we came here lots of cases in the city are rising up, our whole team is here but Sir Simpson is alone, how about we go back?" Brennan asked looking at Noah for confirmation. "I don't think I'll be able to join you after the incident happened here, I can't leave my village like this... Well, I won't stop you two, in fact I would like it if you go there and help him with the cases" Noah smiled as he finished his food.

"So, what do you think?" Brennan looked up at Eve. "I think, we should help Sir Simpson being there with him" she sighed as she glanced at Noah. "Tell him that I'll be on leave for a month" Noah winked at them as if trying to request them to cover up for him.

"Well, if we are talking about Sir Simon, does anyone know what's that, he been busy with and how much load of work he must be facing?" Noah grinned. "He never wants to look weak in front of others...maybe that's why he didn't request us to come back even if he would've been facing loads of work on his own" Eve chuckled. "He's surely a man of his words" Brennan smirked playfully as he went outside to attend some call.

"You two can leave tomorrow, I'll book a taxi" Noah smiled as he retired to his room leaving Eve alone in the living. She was bored so she went upstairs to do some packing stuff.

CHAPTER TWENTY

OVERLY INDEPENDENT

It was the next day, finally getting off the cab and walking towards there office, it was relief for them. After spending some days in Mist woods, they surely were relieved at the sight of their normal life hugging them back again. But this time, it wasn't so normal being here again. Everything seemed a little change, "Cool design!" Brennan exclaimed as he looked around their newly upgraded headquarters.

After greeting some of the members, Eve finally turned her way, heading towards cafeteria. There she saw a man sitting with his back facing her, coldly. She looked at him trying to guess his identity as he wore a black woolen overcoat, with his hair, a true mess! She tilted her body to right, trying to see the face hiding behind.

"You guys are back?" the man suddenly caught a glimpse of Eve from the corner of his eye as he stood up and turned around, Simpson! Yeah, it was him, but his tired eyes and weak body was making it difficult for Eve to guess the figure correctly. Her eyes widen at the small surprise she got there, "Oh yeah! we just came back... but how have you been sir? I mean, you don't look fine" she stutters a bit.

"Ahh, I was just working overtime for some days now" he chuckled, smiling weakly as his smile hit the corners, it depicted lines on his cheek.

By the mere look at his face, Eve could tell he wasn't fine at all! He just became overly independent. This man surely had some ego and never wanted to ask for help on his own, it was his team members who helped him through toughest times of his job. No doubt he'd been a punctual man, which helped him getting his own team to head over, but sometimes, he just doesn't cooperate with other team members. He's always ready to complete his tasks even if he doesn't get any help, or maybe he doesn't ask for it!

"I see... you really have messed up sleep cycle!" Eve was maintaining a casual look with her taunts. He smiled a bit but then ignored her taunts, he never wanted anyone to care about his schedule or personal matters, he believed that, asking for help can make him look naive in front of others or it could affect his bossy personality.

The only quality he lacks, while being a leader was surely not cooperating and discussing his work, he always minds his own business and never wanted anyone to mind it for him. He somehow, lacked communication skills, lacked the quality of admitting if he can't do any work by himself.

"where's Noah?" he asked, walking towards trash can to throw his paper cup of coffee. "Uhm, he's on leave" she sighed softly, already prepared with the excuses. "Okay" he mutters as he walked outside spotting Brennan, they both began some conversation. She stood there watching them talk as her chains of excuses weren't of use now.

After submitting some reports she went out of the office, to her home. It was a long time since she came back to her apartment.

She walked inside, unlocking the door, and stepping inside with a sense of relief and comfort. Finally, she was home, away from all the complexity of her life, a day before. She threw her bags away and flopped into her bed. "I don't know how much I missed this place" she chuckled to herself rolling off the bed after a few squirms.

"I have the files prepared in my cabin, you can come with me and check on them too. I sent you some of the records via email. I hope you've checked them too! The last case happened some 3 days ago... and the body wasn't found in crime spot. And when we reached the victim's apartment, all we found there was blood spread across the floor, there's no chance the man is alive now."

"Is there any pattern being followed by her?" Brennan's eyes narrowed. "Her...? You mean Andrea?" "Yeah, I did some research on it before confirming this" he sighed pulling out his phone and then looking back at Simpson.

"I sent you my article" Brennan stated before shoving his phone back into his pocket. Simpson nodded as he guided him away through the hallways into his cabin.

As Brennan entered his cabin he looked around, complete mess. "I think you've been working over time lately" he muttered as his gaze met Simpson. He slightly nodded as he went beside his table searching for files he made in recent days about the murder cases in the city lately.

Brennan stood there watching every detail of his cabin closely- a coffee mug, messy table with too many papers to handle. He gently swiped his finger across the wooden table and lifted it up to his eye-level. "Forgot to clean, huh?" he chuckled as he looked down at Simpson, who was still searching his work between piles of files and records. After sometime Simpson finally stood up, with a yellow folder in his hands as he threw the folder on his table, indicating him to sit down.

"Well, you've 5 minutes... just go through them once and tell me your opinions" Simpson frowned looking at the wall clock and then back at him. Brennan paused for a while before starting to go through the pages. His fingers gliding over the pages turning them continuously, trying to find the main idea and common evidences among the cases happening recently. He studies all the reports thoroughly before looking up at Simson.

Time went by, hours passed, and they both were still discussing the recent murder cases. "How's Andrea's family been, these days?" Brennan asked leaning back into the chair, trying to divert his mind from the murder complexities. "You mean his father?" "Yeah, and I think she had a brother too?" he asked casually not even glancing at Simpon.

"As per the information, his father's in depression after his wife passed away... and his brother is still in some hostel far away from this city" Simpson tried to recall details he was informed about days ago. "Any information or conclusion about his wife's suspected murder?" Brennan leaned in, on the table, this time getting serious in their conversation. "Miss Rachel gave that part to another team, so that our teams work together in different roots of the common case." he sighed in frustration.

"So, she does believe us now? And she should! Because we aren't joking around with Andrea right now!" Brennan breathe in sharply. "Uhm... Noah won't be coming for a week or two-" Brennan suddenly changed the topic. "I know that, Eve already informed me" he replied cutting off his sentence in between.

For some moment there was an uncomfortable silence in the room, Brennan was getting out of words as he was expecting some news from Simpson while he was away.

"Mike Lewin is not agreeing on meeting his regular psychologist" Simpson continued "I think Eve can handle a little counselling session with him tomorrow" "Uhm... okay, I'll inform her" Brennan nodded as he stood up and collected some papers "I think you need some rest too, I'll be get going" he smiled politely and then started walking towards the door, as he reached the door knob he looked behind before walking out completely "And don't work extra hours tonight, your eyes seem to be intoxicated by that messed up sleep schedule, I think you've been following recently" he winked at Simpson and chuckled as he walked away.

CHAPTER TWENTY-ONE

COUNSELLING SESSION

As the time passed, finally Mike entered the cabin, he was accompanied by the nurse who has been taking his care for days. Eve smiled at him as he approached near the table, "Sit down, easy there boy" she indicated him, as her polite smile followed the suggestion. She then turned towards nurse and signaled the nurse to move out.

She then sat on her seat as she looked up at the shivery and cold figure sitting in front. "Is something's wrong?" she raised an eyebrow. "N-no" he stuttered, by his uncomfortable answer and body language, Eve knew he was hiding something. She started off with some normal conversation and questions, about why he isn't eating or sleeping properly? Or why doesn't he communicate with anyone? Was he scared of something?

As she asked the last question, he suddenly nodded and spoke with a shivery tone "Miss, you remember when I had a dream about Andrea?" he stutters a bit.

"Yup! Of course, I do remember that" she started getting hint of honesty. "I still have dreams" he fidgeted with his fingers looking down. "About her? Or some scary dreams which are often due to mental health problems and past traumas?" she leaned on the table. "I-I've seen her killing some people" he began shivering as he continued "she's a monster! She kills and eats humans!" he cried out shivering badly. "Hey do you need water?" Eve suddenly got up from her seat and went to grab some water for him.

"Here, drink this!" she offered him some water as she sat down at her place again. "Can you see their faces?" "Y-Yeah, but I haven't seen them, never!" he gulped in hard, putting away the glass. "So, you don't know any of the people being murdered in your dreams in real life?" he shook his head in denial, shakingly. "Can you tell me when did you have the last dream?" she asked. "f-four day ago" he quickly replied.

Eve knew she would terrify the boy if she asks some more questions on that topic so she pulled some fun segment before ending the session. "I would like to see you again" she smiled as Mike waved her a good bye and went home with the nurse.

As he left Eve suddenly called Brennan and asked him to come with the reports of murder victims from past 3 months. After some while, Brennan walked in with some files in his hands as he sat down in front of her table. "Tell me, how did the session go?" Brennan raised an eyebrow as she wasn't speaking anything for some time. "Well, I think you know about Mike Lewin's precognitive dream?" she started off the topic.

"That dream, which he had just before the night of his father's accident?" Brennan asked to confirm his doubt. She nodded slightly "The boy told me he's been dreaming again... about her murdering people" she sighed. Brennan was quiet for a while before speaking, he processed out the situation in some time. "So, you think those can be precognitive dream too?" he asked.

"For confirming that I asked you to bring files of murder victims, I think we could send their pictures to Mike, if he identifies anyone from his dreams, we can consider our doubt to be real" she held out her hand, taking the file as she picked out her phone and clicked photos of two random victims and then sent them with some text.

"Can you tell me the date of last murder case?" she shoved her phone inside her pocket looking up at Brennan who already began searching for the date in files. "Some four days ago..." Eve's eyes widen in sense of realization as she began recalling the exact time being told to her by Mike too. He also mentioned the same night when he had the last dream. "Something wrong?" Brennan asked. "I asked the boy about when he had his last dream about Andrea! He told me the exact day!" Eve frowned snatching the file and confirming the date by herself. "If that's so, it means that boy really does hallucinates the murders being played in his dreams on alternate days, and that too on the days of crime itself!" Brennan began realizing the situation slowly. "The team didn't find the dead body of the victim, maybe he can tell us about the disappearance or anything related to that?" Brennan placed his hands on the table supporting his shoulders.

"You mean, another counselling session?" Eve asked, her question followed by a slight nod of Brennan. "I don't think he can answer such questions, the mental trauma has been destroying his brain and health. Though, we can ask him some random and less explicit questions" she suggest her opinions.

"You sent him the photos, right?" "Yeah" "Then tell me his response, if it's positive, then call him for another counselling session and if it's not, then maybe he's just having bad dreams" he picked up his files and phone as he walked out without even glancing back at her.

133

CHAPTER TWENTY-TWO

Uninvited Guest

She left the office after some 2 hours of submitting her pending forensic reports, "no driver available! That was the least I could expect at this hour" she muttered to herself in frustration as she began walking through the cold streets, she pulled out her phone and began watching some articles while walking down the streets.

Suddenly she felt like she bumped into someone, but as she looked up "sorry" huh? No one was there! She looked around to see what happened to collide with her, but there wasn't even a single human or any car. She felt scared more than anything, she stopped there for a while, never realizing her phone slipped off her hand. "Ouch!" she suddenly bent down to pick up her phone as she saw some green-dot like reflection on his phone's screen.

"An eye?" she thought to herself before looking in front of her, the view made her crawl back on ground few inches away, breathing heavily as the air hung heavy around her, it felt like her heart skipped a beat as she saw the same cat again! Black, green eyes and the same scar! It was her! it was her! Her mind raced with uninvited thoughts of disbelief as she felt shivers running down her spine.

She suddenly picked up her phone and started running away as fast as she could, no matter how breathless she got with each long stride, she never stopped. Looking back repetitively as she saw the cat tilting her head as it watched her running away. Her body started to get stiffened as she ran continuously cutting through cold breezes around her. Never wanting to look back she reached the headquarters, back again. She started pulling the door continuously, "Locked, shit!" she began crying to herself in haste. But she never stopped as she began knocking and yelling loudly so that the guards could hear her cries from outside.

She continuously shouted knocking on the door louder than ever before as she kept on checking her back, not wanting to see that guest again. No one opened the door, panting heavily she saw the restroom, located outside the main building, without wasting any moment she got inside locking the door behind her as she slid down the door breathing heavily, tears never stopping in her eyes.

She slowly squatted near the wall as she pulled out her phone and started dialing to Brennan, her hands shivering badly. "Please pick up, please pick up the damn phone" she chanted to herself hoping the bad time passes as soon as possible. Finally, he picked up.

"Hey?" his tone was sleepy as if he just woke up.

"Please h-help me" she began trembling and sobbing on phone, her voice was shivery, she tried to keep her voice low not wanting the cat to come here, but failing every second on it.

"Calm down, calm down! What happened? Where are you?" he started to get into his senses.

"I-I am at the office, please just help me this time!" she begged as she began crying, getting breathless.

"But what happened?"

"The cat's after me, she found me!" she cried more trying to catch breath as she chokes on air continuously.

"Hey listen, stay there! I'm coming, okay?" he cut the phone and rushed downstairs with his car keys, he didn't even know what to do or what situation is going on there, all he had was just random clues and place. But the question was, how did she end up there? Crying so bad as if she's begging for life! He drove his car as fast as possible trying to reach her, she was surely too soft-hearted if the reason comes out to be some lame prank or random cat.

His mind raced with different kind of thoughts, his vision still a little blurry, because he just woke up from the bed and started driving without even washing his face, maybe he was too worried after the random midnight call, and that too in some crying and shivery voice. 'Something's surely not okay with her' he thought to himself driving the car as fast as he could.

As he reached in front of headquarters, he got off from his car not even caring if the car was parked in middle of the road. He rushed towards the door but it was locked, his hands reached his scalp as he scratched his head in frustration and concern. Just then, he heard some sobs coming out of the women restroom, Eve. He ran towards the door and knocked it impatiently, "Eve, you there?" he asked raising up his voice allowing the person inside to hear him clearly.

Suddenly Eve opened the door, without wasting any moment she pulled him inside and locked the door again, with soaked cheeks and puffy eyes, he could easily tell she's been crying for a while now. "What-" before he could complete his sentence, Eve hugged him tightly not wanting to let go as she cried her heart out on his shoulder, "Hey!

Stop crying! What happened?" he slowly patted her head trying to look down at her.

"Shh... It's okay, but at least tell me the reason!" Brennan raised his voice so that she could hear him between her crying session. "T-the cat" she kept chanting the word in between her sobs. "So, you saw the same cat?" Brennan tried to console her. She nodded, still hugging him tightly.

"See, it's not here now! Stop crying for god's sake" he pulled away as she wiped off her tears with her palm. "Ah, just look at this!" he chuckled indicating towards his shirt which was all wet around the shoulder and chest. She chuckled too, her emotions mixed with past trauma and the lame act being played in front of her right now.

"Should we go and discuss this later, or maybe the next day?" Brennan asked, tilting his head. "Are y-you sure the cat wasn't anywhere when you came here?" she stutters a bit. "Uhm... I don't think I saw anything suspicious" he cleared his throat as he turned around to open the door.

They both came out as he led her towards his car, "What were you doing here this late?" he began as he sat down in driver's seat. "I was just walking to home. You know how problematic it gets when you don't bring your own vehicle to office." She sighs as the engine started filling up the silence between them. She looked down at her fingers as she fidgeted them through the whole drive. Her mind still recalling the things which happened that night. But a question still hung heavy in her mind, who was the one she bumped into accidently?

"Do you have any boyfriend?" Brennan cut through her thoughts "huh?" she was too numb to answer that random question. "I asked because I thought I could drop you with someone you know, or should I drop you at your place?" Brennan stated, his eyes still fixed on the road. "N-no I don't have one" her reply made Brennan's eyebrows twitch in amusement, "If you don't have one till now, then I'm damn sure you're going to die single!" he laughed out trying to keep her mind away from the incidents that happened tonight.

She made a face, irritated. She looked out of the window "Just jokes" "I know" she sighed.

After some 5 minutes, the car was now on the entrance of her apartment's building, she got off and waved a good bye and thanks to Brennan as he drove away. She walked inside the elevator, pressing the button of her floor. As she reached there, she pulled out her keys and unlocked the door quickly, got inside, and locked it securely before moving and settling in completely.

'I'm at my apartment, thanks' she texted him as she closed her windows and drew curtains over them, trying to cut off every way for anyone to come in before the night pass. She flopped into her bed, squirming through the hours she couldn't sleep but then felt a little guilty to have bothered George out of his sleeping time, when she very well knows he has insomnia, he can't sleep properly.

Her phone clicked with notification, "Mike?" she muttered to herself as she opened the chat box.

'I know them! One of these men came in my last dream... I'll tell you the rest of the details tomorrow, I got the orders from your office to be present in the next counselling session, thank you for helping me out, I'm feeling much relieved now! And I'm sure somehow, I'll improve my health conditions with your continuous support...'

She smiled at the text, good. Now she knows the boy's been surely having precognitive dreams, his dreams can be very helpful if they're well connected with Andrea and her next victims and murders. Her mind started clicking with ideas and the next milestones they had to achieve in the days to come, the sooner this case gets solved, the better. She can't handle the traumatic surprises she is getting since she's been a part of this game.

She forwarded the same message to her teammates, threw her phone away and cuddled into her pillow. 'Everything will be okay..." she chanted it to get some stable breath and calm mind.

CHAPTER TWENTY-THREE

CALLING HER FRIEND

The next morning, Eve was in her lab, getting some files prepared for attachment. Suddenly a firm knock was audible to her, "Come in" she was focused in her work as she slowly looked up. "Oh boy! Why're you here at this hour? It's too early, I think I remember you were expected to be here at 10 AM, it's only 7" she chuckled leaving her test tubes and papers aside for a second.

"N-no Miss I've to tell you something!" he shook in fear, "you dreamt again?" It was like Eve read his mind. He was shocked for a moment but then nodded. "Who was he? Do you know that guy?" Eve was getting curious as, if this murder happens to be true then the team could probably use this boy.

He nodded his eyes filled with tension, his stiff body explaining every detail in its own way.

"I-It was Clara, Clara Vincent." He stuttered. "But She was her best friend, right?" she raised an eyebrow. He nodded again. "Do you know where she lives?" "I think she lives near St. Abott Anthony, somewhere in neighborhood. I'm sure Alex has her address!" he picked out his phone and texted someone.

"So, you can text me the address later" she smiled as she continued "I'll pay her a visit today itself, when you'll walk out, you'll see a door on rightmost corner of this hallway, that's where Brennan will be meeting you, today he'll be taking your counselling class! Just tell him that I called you early and he won't say anything about your timings"

She watched Mike as he walked away, going where he was meant to answer some tough questions, she doesn't think he's mentally prepared for such rough conversations. She drifted her gaze to her pending work and started working on it again. After some 1 hour she got the address texted on her phone. She messaged Simoson, to ask if he could join her on some case related visit.

She wasn't in hurry, not at all. Because if something would've happened with Clara, the reports must've been submitted to her office. So, it was still a doubt to be cleared, but this could be only confirmed when they pay a visit to Clara Vincent. So, she packed her stuff and kept the remaining work in her drawer as she walked out checking on her phone for Simpson's message.

'Uhm... okay, meet me at cafeteria then'

A sudden text appeared from Simpson's side, her eyes lit up as she looked around in the direction of cafeteria and walked inside, her eyes searching for Simpson, there he is! Sitting in the same corner as before, she approached him. "I thought of visiting Clara Vincent, there are some important questions and doubts about Andrea, I think she may help us... she was her closest friend after all" Eve tried to make him agree on her request, she knew she was lying and she didn't have any questions as such, she still insisted on letting the act go as far as it could.

After some common discussion he finally agreed upon going with her to Clara. Her home was a little far away from headquarters so Simpson booked the office's driver for safety and as they were going for office's work too.

Half an hour passed, and here were they both standing before Vincent's villa. It had a beautiful exterior design, unique from any other in the same colony, easy to spot! Eve began walking towards the door as she knocked it firmly, after some time, someone opened the door, it was house maid. "Yes?" the lady asked rudely. Simpson showed him his police ID. "We wanted to have a little chit chat, if you don't mind" Simpson kept a straight face, directly staring into the lady's soul through her eyes.

"Where's Clara Vincent?" Eve asked leaning in forward. "She must be sleeping in her room" the maid hesitated a bit. "Are you sure she's in her room?" Eve's eyes narrowed to confirm if she really, was safe. "Yeah, where would be she, if not in her room" the maid smirked. "Ah, right" Simpson cleared his throat. "Can you call her out?" Eve stepped in front of the lady.

"O-okay" she stuttered a bit, as she opened the door completely, signaling them to come inside and have a seat, she then, went upstairs in Clara's room. They both sat on the couch placed in middle of the living room. They waited for some time, looking towards the stairs waiting for them to show up. Suddenly the maid came down running and panting.

"S-She's not in her room!" she breathes heavily her hands pointing towards Clara's room. Eve suddenly stood up and rushed in the direction, the lady pointed. As she reaches the door, her hands reach the door knob, as she pushed it open. The lady was right, she's not here. Her bed was undone and room, a complete mess. She looked around the whole room, turning around, she looked at the lady who was now standing in front of her. "Are you sure Clara isn't anywhere else?" "Yeah! she never goes out without telling me, she doesn't wake up this early usually" The lady maintained her scared posture as she tilted her head to take a glimpse at her room.

"She's not here" Eve sighed. "Where is that girl now?" Simpson break in their conversation. "Wait, I should just check through the room, maybe we can find something!" Eve exclaimed as she stepped inside. At first, she looked around the room and the furniture, her eyes finally fell on the bed, she took a closer look of the sheets. "Ah!" she suddenly bents down to pick up a fur from bed, it was black. She shoved the fur into some plastic mini bag, her eyes roaming around for better and clear evidences.

The room filled with typical teen stuff and closets filled with latest fashion clothes, her eyes wander around the room searching every corner and wall, windows were closed as there was clearly no sign of forced entry or exit.

After some twenty minutes she came out, "I'm sending some cops, you can tell them some details related to her and your last interaction, for now we'll be leaving" Eve informed the lady. "Any evidence?" Simpson glanced at her. "I think I found a string of fur. I'll get the DNA reports this evening, I'll send you the reports and results as soon as they come out"

She knew the fur belonged to the cat, but didn't want to explain the whole situation to Simpson. Firstly, she wanted the DNA reports to prove her point to Simpson, as he didn't seem to be completely convinced with Andrea doing all the murders. In order to reach the climax of this case, she needed a team which cooperates and shares the same type of ideas regarding the problem.

At first Andrea's mother, then Mike's dad and now Clara, these all victims were directly or indirectly connected with Andrea. She murdered several people in between, but still the main question which stressed out Eve was, *'Why's she killing her close ones?'* She sometimes gets her mind soaked into such thoughts deeply. *'She may kill Mike someday too, who knows? And her father? And her bro-, no! she won't kill him, he's not her blood relator, but he too was close to her'*

Her thoughts getting complex and wild as she thinks about Andrea furthermore, she suddenly zoned in. Sitting in the cab, she looked outside the window, it was almost noon. 'I think cops would've reached there by now' she mutters to herself as she pulled out her phone to check some notifications.

Her life was getting darker than before, she experienced a lot in few days. Fear, confusion, panic and haste. Her life was going on smoothly before Andrea's mystery came before her. At first her team was only assigned Andrea's case and now they all were stuck between two stories at a time, she felt a connection between the stories, Andrea's connection to the Mist woods and to every murder case they've been witnessing from the past 3 months. It was all connected, but the strings were tangled. It was all clear but their visions were blurred.

Every time when they thought they found something new, were the times they experienced their reports getting more complex, it all felt like some pieces of stories tied together with thin yet fine strings, which never loosened to let go. They had to mask their tired faces behind their curious one, their defeated faces with ambitious one and so on...

But her thoughts of letting go couldn't take over her mind. Curious, as the human brain is. Her thoughts engaged together into a whole new story cooking up in her mind. In recent days, she spent most of her time either thinking about Andrea or about any other forensic work. It seemed like she was possessed by the uninvited thoughts of Andrea, or was she just curious to know what happens next? Where this all leads to?

CHAPTER TWENTY-FOUR

WELCOME ASHER

After some stressful days, their lives getting replayed every morning, Brennan walked inside the office, wishing good mornings and greetings with a polite smile. The smile was just a mask, he was using to hide how tired and frustrated he was. How much he missed his old chill days and his Sundays which were not followed by piles of work.

He turned towards cafeteria, "Hey, Eve!" he stated raising his voice, waving his one hand in air trying to grab some attention. "Where's Noah?" he asked, sitting in front of her at the table. "Noah? He was coming today?" she asked back. "Yeah! I didn't tell you about this, did I?" "no" she replied flatly. "Uhm... he was supposed to be here by 10, I thought he must be somewhere around but we didn't cross paths, it means he's late again" Brennan sighed pulling out his phone as he texted Noah.

'Where are you buds?'

He looked up at her trying to recall the words he wanted to say "So, I heard Clara Vincent has gone missing? It's been 4 days. Do you have any evidence or clues?" he asked leaning back in his chair. "No details or evidences as usual, and if you ask me, I don't think we'll find any in future too. The mysterious cases of murder and disappearance are all related to Andrea, and she never left trails." She sighed as her eyebrows twitch in sorrow.

'I'll be there in just 5 minutes'

Notification pops up on his phone's screen, sliding away the phone with frustration he looked up at her. "I'll be going with Noah to visit Mr. Holmes today. You want to join us?" "Yeah sure, I'm almost free today" she stretched herself out of the chair, picking up her stuff. "So, when's he coming?" Eve questions. "In some 5 minutes, I hope so" Brennan chuckled as he finished his coffee and stood up too, he started walking away signaling Eve to follow him in Noah's cabin.

"Hey guys!" Noah breath in sharply walking into his cabin as he walked past them to his seat. "Missed me?" "No" "Ouch" he put his hand on his chest mockingly. "So, we have to meet Mr. Holmes today" Brennan looked at him with cold face as he speaks "And you'll be joining us too"

"Work, as soon as I came!" Noah sighed as he leaned back in his chair stretching his arms out of stiffness. "Get your senses together, we'll be leaving in short time" Brennan sighed patting his hand on table as he stood up and walked away. "See you" Eve smiled and left the cabin after him.

'Thanks for your concerns, I've been fine lately... and I've been following the exact schedule the nurse told me to, I think it helped me in reducing stress. I'm so grateful for your support...'

"Good to hear, sir" Eve passed a polite smile. "I heard Asher is home, after so many days?" Brennan kept his tone casual. "How'd he been?" "He's good, I mean better, since he moved out of this place" he replied. "Is it okay if we meet him?" Noah asked, his tone regular. Jonathan nodded as he called out "Asher! Look we have guests!" he yells through the hall and with a split of second he looked back at them with a corner smile.

Asher came down through the stairs, as Noah lifted his eyes to meet the figure coming towards him, he gets startled and suddenly chokes on air, "Uhm... sorry" he cleared his throat, grabbing a glass if water from the table. He couldn't believe what he saw,

'*Same face!? Almost like him when I last saw him, what a great coincidence*'' He thought to himself as he passed a genuine smile too.

"H-hello everyone" Asher stuttered a bit, not expecting so many guests. He forced a smile on his face as he sat beside his father, fidgeting with his fingers. "So, how are your studies going on?" Eve started a casual topic. "It's good" he replied with a low voice.

As the conversation goes on and grew casual among them, Noah was sitting there observing the boy carefully, he was a bit tensed about something he didn't want to admit, not yet. He just sat there watching the boy, he was thinking something so deeply that he wasn't even paying attention to half of their conversation, completely zoned out. His eyebrows were in a line, signifying the look of tension. He tapped his foot on the marble floor rhythmically trying to think straight, and not to get lost in his thoughts.

"Is everything okay, dude?" Brennan asked him with a low tone, trying not to disturb Eve's counselling session. His sudden voice break through Noah's chain of thoughts as he zoned in suddenly with a flinch, shaking up his whole body. "Oh! Yeah!' he suddenly replied as he leaned back in couch trying to concentrate and take notes of their visit.

The time passed by, it was now almost two hours since they came here. "Oh god! When will her questions end?"

Brennan sighed leaning back in the couch, his voice as low as whisper as he turned his face towards Noah. "I didn't know she can talk for two hours straight"Noah replied too as they both chuckled a bit.

'I'm just glad to know that you are doing well now, I know you've been through very bad times, your sister and then, Mrs. Holmes... Good days will surely come and I hope they come soon, I guess we'll be get going now, I wish you two a good luck, for your days ahead!'

"I would like to have a walk with you someday...I hope you don't mind" Noah chuckled as he held out his hands towards Asher. He was numb for a while, like he was deciding his response, finally his words came out "Oh, sure!" he smiled back.

CHAPTER TWENTY-FIVE

KILLER FRIEND

Late at night, Noah was still awake. Working late hours, in his room. His laptop was in front of him, the colors hitting his face in dim light. "Uhm" he finally pulled away, stretching his arms out in air as he looked around to see the time, "1 AM, interesting" he smirked to himself, like he was mocking to himself for this messed up sleep schedule. He picked up his phone, finding a new notification, an audio message? He begun the audio, his phone's speaker now near his ear.

'I know it's too late right now but we need you in the headquarters right now! We've informed the rest of your team about this. They'll be there soon too. The latest report is related to the case we assigned to your team so, it's better if you all come and check this by yourself. It is an emergency, I repeat, it's an emergency'

"I guess I should take early retirement" he frowned as he stood up stretching his whole body this time. He picked up his necessary belongings and some files, in case they would be needing any information or confirmation, and walked out locking the main door behind him.

'I don't know why but sometimes I'm just fed up with this all... I don't enjoy my work anymore! I started this because I

found it interesting, doing things and solving mysteries were my favorite tasks to do, when I was a kid. I know I have to be available whenever they call the team together, but it doesn't mean they'll call us anytime... It's better if it really was an emergency, or I'm going to lose my patience for some work that could wait for later!'

He reached the headquarters after some 5 minutes of driving, as he walked inside, his other teammates were already there, scratching their heads, biting their nails and sweating badly, like something was stressing them out, by the looks on their faces he could tell that they know what was the emergency, suddenly Brennan's eyes lock into his as he reached him with two long strides. "Buds! We have to go right now, get into the car!" he was looking tensed, walking out of the office door, expecting him to follow.

"But what happened?" Noah followed him as he couldn't keep his curiosity anymore. He looked behind as he saw his whole team walking towards a van, a police van. "A dead body's been found near the outskirts of town... our other team went on to check the person, her features resembled like Clara!" Noah's eyes widened as he processed out the situation, Clara's dead!?

As the team reached their destination, they sprang out of the van, rushing towards the crime scene, cops were already there as they reached near the dead body of Clara, now in front of their eyes, they couldn't believe what they saw! It seemed like a nightmare, did Andrea actually murdered her own friend? Or she the creature who killed her only had Andrea's face and not her way of thinking? The case was now getting more complicated with another murder, and that too of her close friend...

The team made their way towards Clara, lying on the ground, lifeless. Her stomach was bleeding and it was scrathed badly, blood was dried, but the amount of blood meant to be found was far more less than average. "Did Andrea s-sucked her blood too!?" Eve's eyes widened as she spotted some bite marks around Clara's neck and wrist. She bent down and collected the flesh sample to check if it was really Andrea or any animal? Some photos were clicked as the team completed some reports as formality and were discussing the aftermaths and possibilities of Clara's body ending up here, and that too, in such a worse condition.

By the marks on her body and scratches all around, it didn't look work of any human, but the bite marks did resembled some human bite-marks.

The team stood there all confused, how can she kill her friend? Oh, but if she murdered her mother too... friend seemed a very short title against it. Andrea's mystery got out of hands as they stood there examining every corner of her body, which was scratched badly, with blood covering her skin.

Did Andrea got out of hands? Or were there no chances that she can be human again?

Epilogue

The team finds itself stuck in chain of incidents and coincidence as the case grew deeper and darker. Can they really know the truth? Or will they end up closing the case...? but they surely couldn't do this, as now, it wasn't just a normal case, it became a part of their lives, every string now connected to them too. Their different perspectives and different believes on the event and stories made their job more difficult.

Read out the next book in this series and you'll find all the answers you want to know about Andrea. About the aftermath... about who she truly is!? and about the lives of the investigation team's members. How it changed and what will they face next? Will they too, find their answers? Or will be left with nothing in their hands? Can they survive from her? Or will they end up losing their lives too? just like others did...

The main question at the end of this book is now- 'Why did Andrea murder her known and close ones? What's her true connection to the village? and how the lives of the people finding about the truth changes?